AN AMERICAN GHOST

An
AMERICAN
GHOST

Chester Aaron

Illustrated by David Gwynne Lemon

HARCOURT BRACE JOVANOVICH, INC.
NEW YORK

For Willy van der Schoot Abbink,
Who Discovered California

It is usually called the mountain lion. It is often called cougar. Or puma or panther. At the turn of the century visitors to the western mountains and deserts, impressed with the animal's ability to move in and out of shadows without being seen or heard, called it the American ghost.

AN AMERICAN GHOST

A FOREWORD

"Can't believe it's Indians," Albie's father said. "Indians wouldn't leave all them tracks. And bare feet. I'm sayin' it's not Indians."

"Course there's tracks," Sam Abernathy said. "Not even Indians gonna move three cows without leavin' tracks. Bare feet. Just one of their tricks. Lookit them dogs, will you. They *smell* Indians. Simple as that."

The two mongrels, Judy and Devil, had been scouting the land ever since they'd left the Abernathy farm. They'd flushed several coveys of quail and a few deer, but their chase had been brief and listless. Now both dogs were racing down the draw, baying at the ground.

"Slaves," Albie's father said. "They been slippin' up the river more and more. That explains the bare feet."

"Indians," Sam Abernathy said. "But it don't matter none. Slaves or Indians, they steal our cows, they get shot. Simple as that."

The baying changed pitch and volume, and as if it had been the signal he'd been waiting for, Sam Abernathy urged his big bay stallion forward. Albie's father clucked his tongue and put Autumn into a canter. Albie let Summer take the bit, knowing she'd been waiting for a run all day. Her body shot forward, heaving between his legs. His head fell back as she moved into full gallop.

Sam's black stallion leaped a fallen tree, and Autumn, close behind, with Albie's father huddled low, followed. Albie again let Summer choose her pace and time. He felt her pick up speed, and as she gauged the distance and bunched her muscles for the jump, he readied his body. Then he was up and drifting and over, and down hard, almost off the saddle but catching himself in time and pressing his body to hers as she carried him through a grove of birches. "The dogs got 'em," Sam called.

Without pulling in his stallion, Sam drew his rifle from its scabbard. Seeing his father draw his, Albie caught the reins in his left hand and reached his right hand down to loosen the buckskin thong and withdraw his own Sharpes. He bent low again over Summer's neck. The branches whipped his body, and he squinted to keep his eyes from watering. He tasted the wind cold and sharp as a knife blade in his open mouth and against the back of his throat.

"Ol' Judy and Devil got 'em," Sam shouted, and the words echoed inside Albie's head: *Got them, got them, we got them.*

Summer broke clear of the birches, and with the ease and grace of a long-winged bird, she took a water-filled ditch and without losing stride carried up a slope and onto the level and into the flat meadow.

Albie saw them then: two figures running through the hip-high grass. Albie's father raised his rifle, but Sam shouted, "The dogs, don't shoot the dogs," and Albie's father lowered his rifle as Judy and Devil leaped to pull the two men down into the grass.

Shouts from Sam and his father mingled with the snarls and growls of Judy and Devil as Albie pulled Summer up hard, his rifle ready.

When Sam and Albie's father pulled off the dogs, the two men remained on the ground. Both sleeves of the jacket of one man had been torn away, and both arms were bleeding. One of the men held a wet red hand to his throat. Albie had seen pictures of runaway slaves in the newspapers that had managed to find their way to the farm, and these men were so dark he thought at first they were slaves. But when, on command from Sam's rifle signal, the men stood up, he saw they were Indians. And young, a year or two older than he was. Fifteen, maybe sixteen. Their trousers and jackets were now ripped and torn even more than they had been before the dogs had gotten to them.

"There's your slaves," Sam Abernathy said with a laugh.

The two men seemed to be unaware, or unconcerned, about their various wounds. They stood with their arms at their sides, their heaving chests the only parts of their bodies that moved. And their black eyes, which shifted from Sam Abernathy to Albie's father and to Albie. Shifted, hovered, and shifted with an indifference that was almost contempt.

"Look at them moccasins," Albie's father said. "Hardly any soles left on them. Pretty sick-lookin' couple of braves, I'd say. They look like they ain't et for a couple weeks."

"And they ain't gonna eat again," Sam Abernathy said. "Simple as that." The two Indians watched, not even their eyes moving now as Sam raised his rifle.

They left the bodies in the high grass. Albie's father argued with Sam about the Indians being buried, saying they might have been baptized, they might very well be Christians. Sam Abernathy said if Albie's father had a shovel hid up there on his saddle, he'd be glad to help dig the hole. But a man did need a shovel to dig a hole. It was as simple as that. His father agreed that well, they ought to at least look for rocks to cover the bodies. Sam agreed, and the three of them searched the grass for suitable rocks but gave up after a few minutes.

With the help of Judy and Devil the three cows were collected and moved toward the birch grove.

16

Albie, tying his scabbard, looked up when his father indicated the darkening sky. When he glanced back, to see the sky growing even darker, almost black, he saw the first buzzard circling high and then drifting down and then gliding into the spring green grass.

CHAPTER 1.

Albie put the second pail of milk next to the first and decided to reward Daisy and Violet with another forkful of hay. He stopped the lift of the fork in midair and turned to gaze down through the barn. He did not move, did not breathe.

Had it stopped?

As he leaned the fork against the post, the tines bit into the soft, dung-soaked planks. Back in these sweet-scented shadows, with Daisy and Violet chomping their

19

hay and snorting and shifting their hooves, with the chickens clucking and scratching and pecking at the planks, it was impossible to know for sure if the rain had stopped.

Shep was gulping down chunks of the heart and liver Albie's father had torn from the cougar he'd killed that morning, but as Albie carried the two pails of milk toward the door, Shep deserted his food to rush down through the dark barn. The chickens scattered, clucking and flapping their wings. Big Red, the rooster, his five-fingered crimson comb held erect, not only refused to run but charged Shep, dipping his head and raising it high, bristling his ruff of red feathers. When Shep ran past, ignoring him, Big Red made a brief pretense at chasing after the hound and then strutted about, reminding his harem he'd once again saved them from disaster.

At the door, Shep waited at Albie's side, anxious to follow him to the milk house, to the cooler sunk deep in the hillside, or to wherever else he was planning to go. When Albie placed the pails on the floor, near the open doorway, Shep took advantage of the delay. He raced back to his food, sending the hens flapping and cackling and forcing Big Red into a repeat performance of his prowess.

Yes, the rain had stopped.

For four days, from sunrise to sunset and with a whistling wind throughout the night, the rain had fallen with that dull, ominous waterfall sound that never varied in pitch or tempo. Now, finally, it had stopped.

Albie stepped into the mud that sucked at his knee-high boots. Behind him the chickens cackled and flapped again. Shep darted past, stopping only to be sure Albie did not turn back.

The rain had not only stopped, but the sun was also trying to fight its way through the low, soggy clouds. The black western sky, as Albie watched, was converted into gray and the gray to speckled gray-pink. It stretched across the western horizon, on top of the far surface of the brown ocean, curled between sky and water, like the upturned belly of a mammoth trout.

Albie reached the bank above the river. River, not ocean, though it stretched away like an ocean, without a distant bank, without a tree or a bridge or even a boat to break the view. As his father had done hundreds of times over the years and as he and Shep had done five times each of these past four days, Albie now picked his way down the path to the oak stake.

Ten years ago, in the same month, March, and just about the same day, the seventh, the river had crested where the oak stake entered the ground. He'd been four years old then, almost five, but he still recalled details of that day: the tattered cap on his father's shaggy head; the faded trousers tucked into black boots; the stern command, "You stay up there on that bank, Albie; don't you come no further." Two days later, in from an inspection of the river, his father had said to Albie's mother, "The storm's over. It ain't rained for twenty-four hours almost, but she's still rising. All that snow melting. You better pack things you don't want to leave behind. I'll get Star hitched to the wagon. Just in case."

Albie and even Elizabeth, a year younger, had helped load the trunks and boxes and a few of the more precious pieces of furniture. Albie and Elizabeth, both fully dressed, had finally fallen asleep in front of the fire, but their mother and father had stayed awake all night. Every twenty or thirty minutes Albie's father had gone into the darkness to inspect the river. After one trip, near dawn, Albie had awakened to hear his father say, "She's going down. I think we're safe." Eight hours later the river had dropped three feet, and by the next evening it had dropped another four. That evening they'd unpacked the wagon, and Albie's mother had made what his father had called "an early Thanksgiving dinner."

In the summer Albie could walk down the path from the top of the bank, past the stake, across the cracked mud flats to the foaming edge of the river in fifteen minutes. Today he passed the stake and reached the river, flowing fast now, with an angry growl, in less than five minutes.

The river stretched beyond where, yesterday, a row of young willows had lined a swelling sandbar (the willows were gone now), stretched beyond where the docks and boats and eight white houses, yesterday, had disappeared between his first and second inspections. Between where he now stood and the speckled belly of that mammoth trout there was nothing but water, nothing but that ocean-river flowing under that persistent growl that shook the ground beneath Albie's feet. Nothing but, at that moment drifting into view, a floating tree, rolling and rocking as the conflicting currents beneath the surface chewed at its various root and branch extremities and sought to swallow it under. Two limbs, reaching up through the viscous brown surface like the arms of a drowning man, clutched at the sky and then, as the tree surrendered to the major current and rolled over, disappeared beneath the brown, growling flatness.

A shack, three white hens roosting on its peaked roof, bobbed along behind the tree, moving closer, falling back, moving closer. Albie continued watching until the tree finally snatched the shack (the hens leaped and ran back and forth and then settled again), and then both the shack and the tree dissolved into the belly of the speckled trout.

On his way back, Albie stopped at the oak stake. He rested his hand on the top, his fingertips caressing the deep impressions made by his father's heavy sledge ten years before.

Today was Tuesday. They'd be home tomorrow. At least his father would be home. If they were still needed at the Abernathys after tomorrow, his mother and Elizabeth would remain a few more days and would keep Alice Anne with them. But in three or four days they'd all be home.

He could admit now that yes, he'd been frightened. But with the rain stopped and the sun coming out and with his father coming home tomorrow, he was safe.

After the last four days, Albie decided, he could do just about everything there was to do on the farm. Had his father really been as confident as, four days ago, he'd declared he was? The youngest Abernathy girl had appeared that day, bearing the almost illegible note that told of her father's injury. Albie's mother and father had prepared to return with the girl immediately.

"I'll be there three nights," his father had said. "Maybe four."

"I'll probably stay longer," his mother had said.

Albie had managed to pretend unconcern. "You can both stay longer," he'd said. "I'll be all right. Don't hurry back just on account of me."

His mother had assured him that they'd not be hurrying back on account of him. The Abernathy boys had promised to be there in four days and would then relieve Albie's father. If their wives came with them, Mary Abernathy would be in good hands. "But they got their work to do, too. If they don't come, I might stay on a while. It's a bad time for Samuel to break his leg, with Mary still so weak and the children still so helpless."

Albie studied the river one last time and then started back to the house. He hummed to himself, trying to recall his father's song. "On Canaan's shore . . . on Canaan's shore . . . " He laughed and raced Shep to the house. If his father had not truly been confident four days ago, he would be, or could be, from now on.

In the house, Albie added a large oak log to the fire. The flames seemed to crackle with special energy, with greater heat. He cut the last shreds of venison from the roast his father had brought him the second morning, and then, with the bone, he lured Shep onto the back porch, where the dog grabbed the bone and carried it off toward the barn. There, even Big Red would be intimidated by the menacing sounds of crunching jaws.

Albie disposed of the venison along with two slices of thickly buttered brown bread his mother had sent this morning. From one of the two storage closets, stocked from floor to ceiling with jars of vegetables, fruit, rabbit, and venison, Albie chose a pint of stewed tomatoes, which he ate directly from the jar. After tonight, with his mother home, he'd no longer be permitted such behavior. To eat from a jar or a pot or to eat standing up was, his mother argued, the manners of a pagan, and she would have no pagans in her house. Well, despite such irritating restrictions, he was anxious to have her here, ordering him to wash his hands and comb his hair before he came to the table. He chuckled to himself, pausing near the sink to try to remember if he'd washed his face or combed his hair once since they'd been at the Abernathys.

After he stacked the dishes in the iron pan, Albie removed his boots and lay on the rug in front of the fire. He'd rest for just a few minutes before going out to make sure the animals were settled for the night and the barn doors were bolted.

Staring up into the beamed ceiling, at the shifting patterns of shadows within the thrust and cross of the beams, lying there with the heat from the crackling fire on his body, Albie fought against the temptation to sleep. He forced himself to run over a list of chores he might have forgotten, but he assured himself he'd completed all the chores his father had suggested. Tomorrow, after the outside chores, he'd wash the dishes and clean the house, or at least that part of the house he'd used. How clever he'd been not to use his bedroom upstairs but to sleep down here, in front of the fire. Not having used the rooms upstairs, he'd not have to worry about getting them in order. Wouldn't they, his mother and father, be impressed?

Maybe, he thought, he better do the dishes and clean the large kitchen tonight, before he spread his blankets and fell asleep. If they came early, before he finished the chores . . . well, just another minute or two.

The fire roared in the hearth. From the hill above the chicken coops a fox barked. Shep charged out of the barn, baying, and was off, his heavy voice informing Albie, and the fox, that they were in for a long night race. Albie smiled as he yawned. Shep needed the exercise. Late tonight he'd return to the back porch, wet and muddy and exhausted, announcing his presence with two short barks. Then he'd curl up on the sacking near the back door, to keep a delayed guard over the animals and the house.

Albie closed his eyes and listened. This was the first night he did not hear ghost noises, the first night he did not have to keep his rifle at his side. Where was his rifle? He raised his head. There, leaning against the back of a chair. Within easy reach, just in case. He lay back, reassured. He wasn't frightened, definitely not, but he'd sure be glad when they were all home. He listened and heard Elizabeth teasing Alice Anne, and he heard the house ring with Alice Anne's giggles. He'd have to pretend, of course, he'd not even known they were gone.

26

He'd succeeded in feigning nonchalance every morning when his father, as he'd promised he would, had come to talk about possible problems. Not, his father had repeated every morning, to satisfy himself about Albie's competence, but to bring him food and to answer any questions that might have come up after the previous day's visit. It was a two-hour trip, but every morning, after he'd completed the chores on the Abernathy farm, his father had appeared on the muddy road, riding Autumn.

This morning, in the heavy rain, his father had ridden Summer. "With this rain," he'd said, "I didn't want to have to fight that stubborn Autumn all the way. And it was a good thing, I'll tell you. Autumn would have spooked when we met that cougar. But Summer here," and he'd reached down to pat her steaming buckskin neck, "she just stood still and let me get off two perfect shots." He'd reached behind him and, before dismounting, had tossed down the still bloody pelt.

During the next hour his father had examined the animals and the interior of the barn and the house. He'd nodded and slapped Albie on the back. "Wouldn't none of it look any better if I'd done it myself."

Albie had accompanied his father down the path to the river.

"It's coming up pretty fast," Albie had said.

His father had nodded. He'd studied the flat spread of water and then the sky. "If it rains another day or two like this, we're in trouble. If it's still raining tomorrow when I come, we might just have to move out. We can stay with the Abernathys."

27

"But what about those levees, Pa? Weren't they built to hold back floods?"

"I don't know about them levees. I've seen them, but they don't seem like much to me. Just banks of mud. You know what I think? I think this summer we'll pull up and move."

"Move? Where to, Pa?"

"Back further. And up. The top of the hill. We start building in May, we can move in by August. Then this old river can flood all she wants, far as I'm concerned. The Abernathy boys'll help. Maybe even the Hasses and the Wurteles. I've built many a house for friends, and many a barn, too. Now my friends can help me. Your mother's never said a word, but I know. Every year, every spring, I know what she's thinking."

Albie had waited, knowing his father would explain.

"She thinks Pa was out of his mind, building so close to the river. It ain't been too bad, though. Your grandpa built the house in 1830 and it's only been flooded once. I was eight or nine years old. Not bad, once in almost thirty years. But the danger's always there, and your ma knows it."

The fire was dying. Albie threw another log on the flames and, instead of retrieving his blankets from the window seat, he rolled up in the hooked rug. He'd just sleep for a half hour. Then he'd take the lantern and make sure the animals were secure. He didn't have to worry about oversleeping because when Shep returned, his barks, from the back porch, would awaken him.

Albie slept more soundly than he'd slept since the

family had been gone. He slept so soundly that he did not hear the first faint tapping raindrops, he did not hear the tapping increase to a steady fall. And he did not hear the heavy rumble that swelled to a roar as the wall of water that had breached and demolished the levee five miles to the north swept down the river, spread across fields, toppled trees, demolished bridges, swallowed animals, carried entire villages before and under its assault.

The house that had survived almost thirty years was lifted and rotated and tipped almost over and leveled and rotated again.

Albie was screaming as the water poured through doors and windows and cracked walls and up through the shattered flooring. He was still screaming when he at last fought free of the rug in which he'd wrapped himself.

He tried to stand, but the water tossed him back and forth, from wall to wall. His hands and knees, once, twice, scraped rough surfaces he tried to grasp. Then he was on the stairs leading up toward the bedrooms. The water, at whatever step he was holding to, swirled above his waist.

Coughing, gagging, Albie pulled himself up until, on the fourth step from the top, he was clear of the water. Though he knew he was at the top of the stairs, he felt as if he were descending. He waited. If the water was below him and he was escaping it, he had to be climbing *up*. While he waited, thinking, the house continued to shift and rotate, like a wood chip caught in a series of whirlpools.

He could see nothing in the darkness, but he could hear. He could hear the rain falling and he could hear the wind crackling and he could hear the water slapping the walls of the house.

At the top of the stairs, on the landing, he paused to rest. He coughed out more of the water, and he sat with his back against a wall for support. Shivering, clutching his arms around his chest, he tried to make sense out of what had happened. All he could do was shiver and cough.

Albie stood and staggered along the hallway. The first room on the left was his parents' bedroom. He found the door, but it would not open. Farther down the hall, on the opposite side, was his bedroom. The door, open, was hanging by the top hinge only. Inside the room, Albie went to the window. He could see nothing. It was as black outside as it was inside.

He picked his way about the room, stumbling over an upturned chair, tangling his feet in a piece of clothing, until he touched and recognized the heavy oak dresser his father had built last Christmas. The dresser had slid halfway across the room, but it had not toppled over. One of the five drawers had fallen out, but the other four, though open, were still intact. Albie found a drawer filled with heavy flannel underwear and shirts and another containing wool socks and a pair of heavy trousers. He pulled off his own soaked clothing, dried himself with a combination of clothes he could not identify, and drew on underwear and trousers and shirt. Only then did he realize that his boots were gone. He was in his bare feet. He pulled on a pair of warm wool socks.

Finding the chair, he set it upright and pushed it to the window and sat in it, a blanket tight around his body.

He was still too dazed, too exhausted, to think clearly. He dozed, jerked awake, dozed again, awakened again, until he realized that he was staring, fully awake, at the pale gray light that filled the window.

Albie threw off his blanket and ran to examine the damage the water had delivered to the barn.

The barn was gone.

A vast endless plain of water lay outside, flowing, hovering, a foot or two below the windowsill, slapping and sloshing against the exterior walls of the house. From this window the barn was always in full view, but now it was gone—washed away. So was the milk house, so was the smokehouse, so was the toilet, so were the pig pens and the chicken coops. Everything . . . everything was gone. Where all the buildings had been there was only that flat viscous sheet of brown fluid.

The house shook, like a dog throwing off water; it tilted and rotated to the left and rotated back, to the right. A tall grove of poplars drifted by, screened by the rain and the gray morning light. They disappeared.

How could trees remain upright when they floated?

Albie staggered back to the chair. It was not the trees that floated. It was the house. The house, like a boat, with Albie the lone passenger, was floating down the river.

CHAPTER 2

Floating. Floating like a boat.

Albie rushed into the hall. The window at the end of the hall had opened, yesterday, onto a small garden area Albie's mother had reserved every spring for the planting of flowers. There was only the water; there was no freshly tilled soil or green grass or potted herbs. The window had been torn from its frame. The wind drove the rain through the hole in the wall, forming a stream that flowed down the slope of the hall, down the steps

33

and into the water that swirled through the kitchen below.

A second effort to open the door to his parents' bedroom was no more successful than the first had been. Having left his boots down there in the water, Albie walked in his stocking feet to the landing. There was the water, shifting in gentle waves against the walls, three or four feet below the ceiling. Pieces of lumber, jars, bottles, cans, bits of cloth floated on the surface. The rug in which he'd slept last night in front of the fire floated in the middle of the room, humped over, like a dark waterlogged body.

Albie climbed along the inclined hallway, carrying with him a long piece of lumber he'd recognized as one of the columns that had held up the back porch. A piece had been torn from one end of the column, leaving it shaped like a wedge. Using the column alternately as a ram, a lever, and a pry, Albie succeeded in opening the door of his parents' bedroom just enough to peek through. The big bed had slid against the door, and its weight was keeping the door closed. After he forced it open enough so he could slip inside, Albie used the same piece of porch-column to lift and slide the bed. Once he had the door open he worked the bed back against it, so that the bed now kept the door from closing.

Albie was glad his father could not see the room. It was just last summer, nine months ago, that he had carved the holes in the wall and fixed the weights with ropes and set the windows he'd bought the winter before from that salesman from Duluth. Albie, that day the salesman had stopped by, had been permitted to stay up till long past midnight to hear the tales of the man's experiences on the railroads and the steamboats and the stagecoaches. Now those windows, like that night, were gone forever.

Looking through one window and then the other, Albie saw the same brown expanse of water he'd seen from his own room. But then, past the rim of the window that opened to the west, floating faster than his own house, came what could have been either a house or a barn, no more than a hundred yards away, wrapped in looping strands of barbed wire. The building and, within the wire, the bloated body of a cow with all four legs stiffly upright, floated with quiet serenity.

Albie turned away. He crawled across the bed. In his room he'd be dry and out of the wind. He'd not yet examined the two other rooms farther up the hallway, Elizabeth and Alice Anne's room and his mother's workroom, but he'd do that next—after he sorted his thoughts and fit them into some form of plan for his rescue. As long as the rain continued falling, as long as the river continued rising, as long as there was no land in sight, he was restricted to this house, almost to his room.

He was not a very capable swimmer—he knew that too well. Some days, in the summer, in Willow Creek, he could manage to cross the creek three times, dog paddling, without stopping. But even an excellent swimmer challenging this current would be risking death. Summer . . . Willow Creek . . . how far in the past

35

that seemed! His father and Sam Abernathy had talked about damming up the creek this summer so some of the flatland could be irrigated. Well, they now had their dam.

Willow Creek, Albie knew, flowed into the Redman River and the Redman flowed into the Wisconsin and the Wisconsin into the Mississippi. And the Mississippi, he recalled with a chill that infiltrated his warm, dry clothes, flowed into the Gulf and, from the Gulf, into the Atlantic Ocean. Right this minute he could be floating down the Wisconsin, or even down the Mississippi. Whichever, he knew one thing for sure: he was moving toward the Gulf. If, in the next five or six days, he weren't rescued, he'd be out of the Gulf and into the Atlantic Ocean.

Albie left the window, stunned, and wandered up the hallway, staying close to the wall. The floor, which had once been so clean and polished, could not be seen under the brown water that ran ankle-deep from the smashed window to the steps and down the steps to the kitchen below.

When he opened the door of Elizabeth and Alice Anne's room, it fell forward, into the room. He stopped at the entry. It was useless to go inside. The room had been demolished. A corner of the roof had fallen in, and a large portion of the north wall, or what had been the north wall, had collapsed. The two beds, the chairs, the twin dressers, clothes, dolls—everything was soaked or buried under debris. Nothing could be salvaged. Albie gasped at the thought of what would have happened had this occurred when Elizabeth and Alice Anne were in their beds.

The damage was almost as great in his mother's workroom. The window was gone, the door lay on the floor, the spinning wheel and the loom and the long worktable lay in a single pile of shattered wood. What had been strips of brightly colored cloth, to be made into rugs, lay in their crushed baskets, all of the cloth now a dull, wet gray.

Albie returned to his room. How long would he have to remain here? In this room, in this house? How long would it be until the house was seen and he was rescued? Would the house survive the destruction it had already absorbed? Several of the beams downstairs had collapsed. The walls, at many places, had broken away from the frame. A collision with rocks or trees or even a sudden shift of wind might complete the destruction. Even if he were able to swim, he'd be no safer. Unable to see any land, he did not know the direction he might go to escape the river. And even if he knew which direction might be the wisest choice, he'd not be able to overcome the current. He was certain of only one fact about direction: he was moving down a river that would eventually deliver him into the Atlantic Ocean.

A tree floated by, followed by carcasses of cows and horses and pigs and the remains of other buildings less fortunate, less well constructed, than this house his grandfather had built thirty years ago. Could those cows be Violet and Daisy?

Albie left the room and went to the landing. Down

there, in what had been the kitchen, in front of the fire, he and Elizabeth and Alice Anne had sat through hundreds of meals at the long oak table. How many mugs of hot chocolate had his mother made for him there, how many delicious . . . oh, how he'd love to be sitting there now, watching his mother sewing, watching Elizabeth preparing clothes for her doll, watching his father carve a handle for one of his tools, listening to the sounds of little Alice Anne in the crib.

Albie, with a groan, laid his head in his arms.

By now his parents would know that the house was gone, with Albie inside. That was it! They'd know what to do. They were organizing search parties this very minute. They were sending word up and down the Mississippi for people to keep a sharp eye out for a floating house in which a boy named Albie Bancroft was stranded. He had to stay alert, he had to keep constant watch at all the windows. How would he attract their attention? With smoke. But to have smoke he had to have a fire, and he had nothing to burn and nothing to light a fire with. He could only hope the wind wouldn't destroy his shout, the driving rain wouldn't shield the towel or blanket he'd wave.

How had his parents survived? They'd lived and farmed in Indian territory, they'd lived through droughts and blizzards, they'd lost homes to government agents, and, finally, they'd returned to live where his father had started, at *his* own father's home. They'd never admitted defeat or despair. As soon as the rain stopped, probably the very first day, his father would be starting the new house, higher, farther back in the hills. But he couldn't do both. He couldn't direct a search for his son *and* start a new house.

Albie stared down at the space where the oak table had once been, stared not with anger or remorse but with resignation, as if there were nothing incongruous about the lower half of a house being filled with water. Why, as he watched the alien debris floating in the brown foam, did he think of Daisy and Violet? Of Shep? Of Big Red?

Why should his parents, viewing the empty space where their home had once stood, think that a little bag of skin and bones had survived a tragedy that had demolished a structure of heavy beams? The simplest reasoning would prove the inevitability of his death and the improbability of his body ever being recovered. Or, if recovered, identified. There would be no need to waste time and energy on search parties. No need to . . .

What was that?

He'd heard a voice. He was certain. Back in his room, he tugged and pushed and finally managed to open the window. He leaned out as far as he could. Nothing except that dreary sweep of brown, surly liquid sustaining, here and there, a tip of a tree, a portion of a barrel, a corner of a box, logs like the backs of sleeping alligators. Out of the room and at the end of the hall, clinging to an exposed stud, he saw, again, nothing, nothing but the water. The rain soaked his head and face and the wind threw back his call, "Here! I'm in here! In this house! Help!"

Running, and slipping and falling, and sliding along the water-covered floor almost to the landing, he kept calling out, "Help! Help! I'm in here! In this house! Help!"

On his feet, he crawled over the bed in his parents' room and went to the window. There, no more than a hundred yards away, floated a house and, in a hole that had been the upper window, two people, a man and a woman. They were waving their arms and calling in weak voices, "Can you help us? Please help us."

The sound of the voices and then the sight of the two other humans had charged Albie's body with such energy that he leaped and danced about, waving his arms, kicking his feet, shouting, "Thank you . . . thank you . . . thank you . . ." Then he realized, seeing the two people who looked, from this distance, to be older than his grandparents, who looked as if they needed help as much as he did, perhaps more, then he realized that there would be no rescue. His arms dropped to his sides. He fell against the wall. He tried to return their calls, tried to use his voice, but in his disappointment he could only manage a weak flicker of the fingers on his right hand. The old people continued calling. "Who are you? What's your name?"

Albie cupped his hands to his mouth and mumbled and then shouted, "Bancroft. Albert Bancroft. What's yours?"

He heard the sound of their voices, but he could not distinguish words. The wind was not in their favor. They drifted farther apart; their voices could barely be heard. As if by mutual agreement the three of them stopped calling. Remaining at the window, Albie continued watching the house drift farther away. The rain spilled over his head and body, but he barely felt it. An abrupt cross current caught the other house and spun it around until the two old people were no longer visible.

Albie stayed at the window, blinking against the rain. Even by leaning out of the window, he could no longer see the house. He leaped across the bed and sloshed through the flowing water to the end of the hallway. From the hole where the window had been he could see the house again. It came about just enough to display the two people still standing at their own window. Just before it shifted, to turn, to take them from view once more, they waved. Albie lifted his arm. He waited until the house lost its shape, until its shape and color merged with the gray windswept rain.

Back in his room, Albie sat on the bed. He'd eaten nothing since last night, and though he wasn't hungry, he knew that to survive he must eat. But he had no food.

Ah, but he did have food.

Removing his damp clothes, hopping up and down as he fought the buttons, Albie burst out laughing. Why hadn't he thought of this before?

Undressed, his flesh covered with chill bumps, Albie walked through the water and down the hallway, his thin white body almost glowing in the dark, dank air. He descended the four steps. The icy bite of the water took his breath away, but he continued moving down. The water reached his knees, his thighs, his waist. He shoved himself from the wall and began collecting the various jars and cans and tin and wooden boxes floating on the surface of the water. A few of the jars were broken, but most were salvageable and, thanks to the strong hands of his father, who'd given each cap its final turn on the red rubber washer, the contents had remained unharmed. He relayed everything he collected to the landing.

One of the two cupboards was open. Its shelves, now empty, had been filled with vegetables, fruits, rabbit, and venison that had been canned the previous fall. Some of the collection at the top of the landing had been from that cupboard. The door of the second cupboard, a large cooler that had stored the bulk of the family's food, was still closed. With his fingers, Albie followed the edge of the door beneath the water's surface. He found the latch, opened it, and, struggling against the force of the water, pulled the door free. Jars and boxes and cans tumbled out, several striking him on his head and shoulders. He gathered as many as he could, not taking time to examine their contents, and carried them to the steps, moving fast, so they'd not be swept through the holes in the walls and into the open current.

Without taking time to dry himself or dress in dry clothes, Albie transferred his collection from the steps and the landing to his room. He resisted the temptation to argue that he'd stored enough, so he'd not have to enter the water again. He had to be practical. He had enough food to survive for several weeks, but what if he were compelled to remain in the house for *more* than several weeks? The thought sent a chill deep into Albie's heart, but the possibility had to be faced. He returned to the stairs and went down, into the water.

He recovered a large tin box in which, he knew, his mother had stored several loaves of bread and cakes and cookies. The lid was tight. He'd examine the contents later, but he was sure they'd be dry. A water-tight barrel was half filled with slabs of salt pork. He pushed and tugged and rolled the barrel up the steps to the landing. A tightly sealed miniature trunk of wood and leather contained his father's pipes and tobacco. He carried that to safety, too, not because he intended to smoke but because its presence would offer him an aromatic reminder of his father, of his sitting at the fire at night, telling stories, playing his accordion, singing, blowing voluptuous blue smoke rings for Alice Anne to poke her pudgy pink fingers through.

On those shelves he could reach and in the few drawers he could open, Albie found bits and pieces of things for which he might . . . who could predict? . . . discover a use. The large ball of strong cord his mother had begun collecting before he'd been born. A wooden sewing box filled with thread and needles and two pairs of scissors. Three forks, a spoon, a table knife were all that remained of the prized set of silverware his mother had inherited from her mother. Albie took them all. Just in case, some day . . .

His arms, finally, could not complete another stroke. Both hands were so numb that they could no longer

43

close around an object. His feet were blue, his chin and mouth trembled, his teeth chattered. He gagged on a mouthful of water and wrapped his arms around a post still supporting the handrail. He endured a coughing spasm and then dragged himself up the stairs.

Before he could carry even one of the many objects he'd recovered, he had to get dry, he had to get warm. In his room, he rubbed himself with a wool blanket. He pulled on red flannel underwear and a pair of trousers his mother had made from cloth she'd woven from wool she'd spun, a full cloth so dense and thick it was almost waterproof.

Dry and warm once again, Albie felt better. Rolling up his trousers and sliding up the legs of his underwear, he carried the rest of his salvage to the bedroom. Now, perhaps, he could relax. And he could eat.

He managed, after much exertion, to open a pint jar filled with rabbit meat. He also opened a jar of green beans. They were not his favorite vegetable, but, he thought, he had better get used to eating such food.

Lying on his bed, Albie ate all the rabbit and about a third of the beans. He drank the juice and closed the bean jar as tightly as he could manage. Lying back on his bed, he listened to the water slamming the outside of the wall against which his head was resting. The rain, the ever present rain, continued its steady, drumming fall. The gallant old house, still resisting the attacks of wind and rain and current, could only creak and sigh and groan in protest.

Should he try to build a raft? How would he do it?

He had no tools, nothing with which to secure one board to another. Anyway, why consider building a raft? The house itself was a stronger and more comfortable boat or raft than he could manage to build.

Rescue. That was what he had to hope for. But he would have to be on the alert every hour, every minute. After the flood, steamers and ferries and rafts would be sailing the river again. He'd have to be prepared to signal them in case they saw the house and dismissed it as just one more unfortunate victim they could do nothing for. But since there were victims, there would almost certainly be search parties examining every cove and island. All right, he would be ready. If only the rain would stop.

It did not stop. The drumming, drumming, ever pouring rain added its bulk to the ocean of water already spread across the countryside, moving it hourly, daily, over more prairie land, lifting its already murderous crest, drowning more animals, more people, destroying more homes.

He had no choice. He would wait right here, in this room. He had food, blankets, clothing. All that was necessary now was the continued durability of the house.

The rest of the day Albie occupied himself by moving from window to window, searching for the slightest sign of a boat. The carcasses of drowned animals floated by so frequently now that he no longer noticed them. Twice he saw animals swimming; once, a raccoon that climbed onto a floating log and grinned up at him, and then a large buck, its antlered head up out of the water, swimming toward what appeared to be a floor of a house or barn.

Near dusk Albie completed his final tour for the day. He lay on his bed and tried to convince himself that the rain was not falling as hard as it had been. The house rocked and swayed with the current. As he drew a blanket over his body, he thought he heard voices. He listened and sat up, but each time he traced the sound to the collision of jars or pots in the water below, or to the boards of the house as they strained against the flood.

Drummed to sleep by the rain and the whispering wind, Albie listened with relief and gratification to his mother's praise of his housecleaning, to his father's proud commendations for his care of the stock, to Elizabeth's taunts about his uncombed hair, to Alice Anne's infectious giggles. He was eased out of his dream when the house struck a log, or a series of logs. Several dull thuds rippled through the flooring and up through the bed. A violent crash, not a dull thud this time, plucked him out of his bed and threw him across the room. A giant hand seemed to be scraping its long nails the length of the roof and along the walls, probing for a crack to use as a grip with which to tear the building apart.

The side of the house in which Albie's parents' bedroom lay sounded as if it were collapsing. The treasure he'd brought from the kitchen slid from one end of his own room to the other as the entire house tilted up and down and up. Jars smashed, the chair fell over, brushing Albie's thigh as it tumbled across the room. One of the four oak feet of the bed collapsed, and the corner of the frame fell to the floor. Then, abruptly: silence. Even the wind dropped to a whisper, to a sigh, to nothing. The rain tapped at the window and stopped.

The house was still drifting, but the floor, Albie discovered, as he stood and very carefully made his way back to the bed, seemed level, almost stable. Safer, more secure.

Albie ran his hands across the soles of his feet. He'd not cut them. He lay down on the tilted bed and drew the blanket up over his body again, to await the next catastrophe. The knots in his tense muscles eased. The silence, the continuing durability of the house, was reassuring. Like a great ship undaunted by even the most ferocious ocean, the house floated on—through the newly risen wind, through the revived rain, through the oppressive darkness.

At dawn, when he awakened, the rain had become a mist. Albie stretched, kicked himself free of the blanket, and sat up. Several jars, he saw, had been broken. He'd have to be careful, walking in his bare feet.

He opened the window and leaned out. No boats, no people, no rescuers. Only the remains of what had once been walls or roofs, fences, wagons, and what had once been horses or cows. Bloated, distorted, water-bleached, one animal was indistinguishable from another.

The opening at the end of the hall offered no hope either. But once there, Albie saw the cause of last night's explosion, or the sound that had been like an explosion. The house had collided with an enormous oak tree and, caught within the grip of several branches, would not be easily released. Had he wanted to, Albie could have stepped through the opening directly onto the trunk of the tree. But the mist, hovering close about the house like a fine cotton shroud, threatened to thicken at any moment. He could see no farther than thirty or forty feet beyond the house. Even the base of the tree trunk was obscured within that cotton mist.

He went into his parents' bedroom. One limb that was as thick as his waist had, like a great battering ram, smashed a large portion of the wall. The same limb, at least two feet thick, ran the length of the room and continued through the opposite wall so that the house was now suspended from it like a piece of washing from a clothesline.

A finger of ice pricked Albie's heart as a growl sounded from behind his back. He had to be imagining the growl—it had to be a trick of the wind. He turned, slowly. It was no trick.

In the corner of the room, behind a net of limbs and branches and twigs and wall boards intricately interwoven to form a natural cage, a mountain lion (called a *cougar*, a *panther*, or *an American ghost*, depending upon who might be cursing it) stood erect.

Restricted by the cage, it could not rise on its hind legs, it could not turn, it could barely lie flat. Even as Albie stared, the lion's paws were tearing at the branches. Screaming, spitting, he struggled furiously to free himself.

48

CHAPTER 3

As the lion tore at the walls of the cage, Albie threw himself back. He landed on the bed and continued moving, to roll and fall off to the floor, on the other side.

When he reached his own room, he kicked at the warped door in a futile effort to close it. He leaped into the closet and pulled that door closed. If the lion merely pawed at the door, it would fall open. The iron latch was finely designed and strongly constructed, but it had not been intended to keep out mountain lions.

After what seemed like an hour but could not have been more than a few minutes, Albie opened the door. An inch. Another inch. Farther. He saw no lion, but he was prepared, at the slightest sound, to slam the door closed.

After he stepped out of the closet, Albie tiptoed across the room, his body coiled for retreat. The spitting and snarling had stopped, but he could still hear an occasional grumbling growl and the sounds of chewing.

What could he do? He had no weapon except that silver table knife. And one other. He returned to search the contents of his mother's sewing box. One pair of scissors was about six inches long. In a struggle with a mountain lion it would be almost useless but better than that knife, which would be no more effective than a spoon.

How, Albie wondered, had the animal entered the house? He had to have been on the tree. Before or after the tree had been toppled by the flood? Had he been forced from his den by the rising water? Had he been in the water when the tree passed him by? Had he climbed into the tree for refuge? How betrayed the lion must have felt when, in a single moment during the night, a tree that had been his refuge had been converted to his prison.

For a moment he had to admit to a strong sympathy for the animal. After all, hadn't the storm also converted Albie's refuge into a prison? But within *his* prison Albie was free to move, and tomorrow or the next day or the day after that he would be rescued. The lion would be killed. By him, Albie (how, he'd not yet decided), or by Albie's rescuers. A mountain lion could not be permitted to return to the land to destroy hundreds of sheep or cows or horses. And perhaps even people. Yes, he'd have to be destroyed. What did it matter then if he remained caged for a day or two?

What could he do, Albie wondered, as he peered through the open doorway, what could he do to insure the lion's remaining caged? Leaning on the bed, prepared to flee, Albie saw that had the tree been one foot forward, away from the wall, the big cat would have had sufficient room to maneuver, to fight its way free.

Panting heavily, the beast settled himself on his belly. He dropped his head, with a heavy groan, onto his paws. Albie backed away, disturbed at the strength of his compassion for the animal. Like a persistent worm, the pity remained, continuing to gnaw at his conscience. He knew too well the sudden sense of desertion, of isolation, of threat the lion must be feeling. Free to roam forests and mountains without limit to his range or power, the lion, imprisoned now, must be feeling his loss even more than Albie was feeling his. For just a moment Albie wondered if there was some way he might free the lion without danger to himself. But then he noticed several of the thinner branches already gnawed and broken and torn away, and a few of the larger branches nearly separated. His pity gave way to fear. The lion, when free, would feel no pity for him.

How long might it take the big cat to complete a hole large enough for his escape? He'd be hungry soon, and with hunger would come the impulse to fight even more viciously for his freedom. Perhaps even now the lion was on the verge of such hunger, such an impulse. If he had food, he might relax, he might settle down and accept his cage. If I had something to feed him, Albie thought, if I could somehow get food to him, he might just stay right there, satisfied, until someone frees *me*.

Back in the bedroom, Albie examined the jars. Should he try the venison? Would the lion eat cooked spiced meat? But even if he would eat it, there was not enough available to feed a mature, starved, and desperate lion for more than a day or two. Then what?

From stories he'd heard from his father and his father's friends, and from experiences he himself had had with wild animals, Albie knew they required freshly killed meat. Fresh blood supplied their salt. Without such blood, or salt, the lion could starve in four or five days.

Why, then, should he worry? He could just let the lion starve to death or die from lack of salt. The simplicity of the solution enchanted him. All he had to do was wait.

But what if, during that wait, the lion, more enraged by starvation, chewed his way to freedom? No, he had to be kept calm. He had to be fed. But how could Albie, on this isolated boat of a house, a house adrift on the Mississippi River, or perhaps now in the Gulf, how could he, without so much as a pocketknife, find fresh meat for the cat?

Fish! Would a lion eat fish?

Albie found the ball of cord his mother had collected. He cut a piece of twenty or thirty feet long, tied the smaller pair of scissors to it for a weight, finally succeeded in bending a pin into a close approximation of a hook, baited the hook with a piece of rabbit meat, and tossed the line out of the window.

The occasional outbursts of snarls and growls and the sounds of branches snapping did not contribute to patience or peace of mind. After the rabbit meat failed to lure any fish, Albie tried venison, and then green beans. One was no more successful than the other.

During the time he fished he was never more than a few feet from the closet, should the lion break free of his cage. When he admitted defeat and pulled in his line, Albie decided he'd better prepare for a siege, in case the lion did break free. He transferred almost all of the jars and cans to the top shelves of the closet and then to a portion of the floor. With the door closed, he would have barely enough room to stand upright.

At the window, Albie watched the wind drive a new storm across the liquid meadow. He listened to the aroused surface water strike at the house, listened as it rested a moment and then struck again. He leaned forward, staring into the storm.

There, about twenty feet away, floating ahead of his house, was a barn, the upper remnant of a barn, with the two miniature iron roosters and cows on the weather vane twirling wildly in the wind. And pacing back and forth along the ridge of the roof, like two little old men, were two goats, one pure white and the other spotted brown and white. They were now so close that he could see their chin whiskers, could hear their bleating above the shrill, whipping wind. Oh, if he had a rope . . . if he could swim well enough to . . . if the water outside weren't so choppy and swift and deep . . . if the barn would only drift closer so he could . . .

If . . . if . . . if . . .

As he watched and wished and tried to prepare plans, it seemed to Albie the two buildings *were* drifting, ever so slightly, closer together. Or was he just imagining that? Would they be drifting apart again? He had to do something. If he didn't try something, anything, those goats would be gone and he would die in this room. Sooner or later that lion, driven mad with hunger, would force himself through his cage. The growls and snarls were already louder, angrier.

He left the room, examined the hallway, and, satisfied, went to his mother's workroom, noticing that now that the house was level, the water was no longer streaming down the hall. In the workroom Albie collected almost all of the cloth strips his mother had been saving. He piled them into two wicker baskets that were still reliable and carried the baskets back to his bedroom.

Working rapidly, he tore each strip in half, along its length, and knotted them one to another, tightening each knot securely, until he had a rope of cloth almost forty feet long. He continued adding pieces, interrupting himself twice to run to the window. He'd not imagined it. The buildings were closer together, separated now by a span of no more than ten or fifteen feet. He could see the long eyelashes of the goats, and even through the heavy rain he could see their little pink tongues loop out when they called. Then they saw him. Excited, noisy, impatient, they scurried back and forth, bumping and ramming each other, pleading plaintively to be rescued. "Don't," Albie prayed, "don't let them fall in the water, God, please don't."

With the final strip tied, Albie estimated the rope to be about sixty feet long. More than he'd need. But what if the cloth tore or the knots loosened? He doubled the rope on itself, reducing its length but increasing its strength. It would be stronger wet than it would have been were it dry. And doubling it would increase its strength even more.

As cold as it was in the room, Albie's face was covered with sweat when he started to remove his clothes. Should he wait a few minutes more, to see if the house would move closer? No. He could not swim well, and he might drown in the rushing water, but he had no choice. He had to take the risk. After tying one end of the rope around his waist and the other end around the sturdy sideboard of the bed, Albie stood at the window. The two goats, panicked, seemed about to climb down the sloping roof and into the water. "No!" Albie shouted, as if they were Shep. "No! Stay!"

Hearing his voice they did pause, but their bleating grew even more plaintive.

Albie hesitated, staring at the rain-splashed water, trying to summon enough courage to act. Those stupid goats were pleading for him to save them, but he intended that they should save him. Dumb goats, stupid goats, couldn't they see that they were doomed if they stayed where they were? While they were *here*, they'd at least be dry, dry and warm, before they . . .

Could he do it? Even if he managed to reach the building, and even if he managed to return, if he got them up through the window and into this room, would he be able to feed them to that lion?

Again: what choice did he have? He had to live. He had to get back home, back to his mother and his father and Elizabeth and Alice Anne. To get back he had to live.

For several minutes the two buildings had moved no closer. In fact, they seemed to be drifting apart. The house had been directly behind the barn fragment, but now the house was moving to the left. He couldn't wait any longer. But he did. With one leg over the sill, his back bent under the base of the upper half of the window, he could not take his eyes from that rumbling water thick as hot taffy. A board drifted past, outracing the house in the rapid current. If he delayed one moment longer, he'd never do it.

Albie swallowed hard, took several deep breaths, and lowered himself. At first he paddled toward the fragment of building, but then he relaxed and let the current carry him.

He could not have stayed afloat another second when he felt, beneath his feet, the rough cedar shakes on the roof. He crawled and scrambled, slid back, climbed and dug with finger and toenails at the surface, tore at the shingles, held to nails and pieces of exposed beam. Then he was at the ridge, with one hand clutching the ridge pole. He lay still, catching his breath, regaining his strength. He drew himself up, slowly, and sat astride the ridge pole. The two goats, prancing and dancing, choked out grunts and squeals of relief and delight as they nipped his hands and his hair and butted him playfully in the chest and back.

After a few minutes' rest, Albie tested the rope, pulling gently at first and then jerking it and then tugging with all his strength. It held. He untied the rope from around his waist and outmaneuvered the white goat and then the spotted one, to encircle their bodies with a cross-halter. He tied the end of the rope, again, around his own waist, and after one deep breath he was in the water, pulling the goats down the sloping roof.

He did not have to swim this time—he simply kicked his feet to stay afloat and hand-walked the rope, against the current, to the side of the house. He had to leap twice to catch the windowsill. After crawling inside, he hauled in the terrified goats. Once inside, shaking themselves and trotting about the room, they seemed unable to believe their good fortune. They celebrated for no more than a few seconds before they started gulping up the remnants of food from the broken jars. Snorting and sniffling, they gobbled up chunks of glass along with beans and tomatoes and corn and apples.

No time to waste. No time, certainly, to permit pity or sorrow or regret to take root.

Leaving the goats to attend to their meal, Albie slid

along the wall of the hallway, to his mother's work-room, fearing that at any moment the lion would come bounding after him. The throaty growls and snarls were even more frustrated than before. The tearing of limbs and branches sounded like a logger chopping away at underbrush. After collecting an armful of cloth strips, Albie hurried back to the goats. Famished, intent on their food, they seemed not in the least anxious about the threatening sounds coming from the opposite room.

Albie untied the white goat and held it by the fur at the back of its neck. The shapely little head came up out of its food just once, to snort its gratitude.

Now . . . how should he kill the goat? The knife was not sharp enough. The scissors! He picked up the larger pair, holding them near the goat's throat, ready to plunge them in. Damn the stupid animal! The least it could do to demonstrate its gratitude was to just fall over dead. Wouldn't it do that for him? For itself? A death like that would be far less painful. No, Albie couldn't do it. And he'd known he couldn't. That, after all, was why he'd gone for the extra strips of cloth.

He pulled and pushed the protesting spotted goat into the closet, tossed in several handfuls of vegetables, and closed the door. He pushed the chair and angled it so the top of its back caught under the latch and helped keep the door closed.

Albie tied six strips of cloth together and wrapped the one long piece around and around the white goat's head, so it covered the eyes like a blindfold. He closed the muzzle with other pieces, which also covered the nostrils. If the idea worked, the goat would not be able to smell the lion.

His humane impulses satisfied, Albie tiptoed across the hall, guiding the goat by its horns. Before he entered the room, he glanced through the doorway. The lion was still in his cage, still on his belly, a mix of low, mewing whines and growls in his throat. The goat's ears twitched, and Albie clamped his hands over them. He'd forgotten about its hearing.

The huge cat leaped to his feet with spits and snarls and one long coughing roar that seemed to shake the house even more than the most violent winds had managed to do. The goat's legs stiffened, and its entire body trembled.

Albie placed his hands on the white quivering rump and pushed it forward. With a short, sharp growl a brown claw shot out of the branches, to strike the goat on the side of the head. The goat fell without a sound. Its legs twitched, and then, still clutched in the curled claw, the body grew limp. The brown claw pulled the white body toward the branches. The head disappeared through the opening and, as Albie watched, horrified, fascinated, the jaws of the lion closed on the white fur throat.

From the doorway of what had once been his parents' bedroom, Albie watched the body drawn, inch by inch, through the branches and into the cage.

CHAPTER 4

Albie no longer thought of the room as his parents' bedroom. It was *the lion's room.*

He could not approach the lion's room the rest of the day. Except for those hours he sat near the window, between the window and the closet, with the closet door always open, Albie lay on his bed, staring at the ceiling. He refused to look at or touch the spotted goat tethered to his bed. When it tugged, working to free itself, or when it came to him seeking attention, Albie lay on his side, with his back to the goat. He could not afford to develop even the slightest affection for the ignorant little beast. To distract it and to keep it from bleating, he fed it small amounts of canned vegetables every thirty or forty minutes.

Another night. Which, he was not sure. The third? The fourth? No matter. He was so despairing of any rescue now that it might as well be the hundredth.

He wasn't concerned about the portion of his food reserve that was being consumed by the goat because he still had at least fifty jars of rabbit and venison, and twenty or thirty jars of vegetables and fruits, along with the salt pork and biscuits and bread. Tomorrow he could go down again to the kitchen, or to where the kitchen used to be, and collect more—if more jars were there, if they'd not floated out through the holes in the walls.

Anyway, he wasn't hungry. Since the slaughter of the white goat, even the thought of food made him sick, as it was making him now.

In an effort to divert his thoughts from food, he worked to discover more attractive subjects. As had been happening more and more, he called up images of his mother, and of his father, of Elizabeth, quiet but efficient Elizabeth, of Alice Anne. Shep. The farm. Every image of Alice Anne always included Shep. Poor Shep. He'd been a fat little ball of gray fur when, on the morning of Albie's eighth birthday, he'd found the pup tied to the foot of his bed. They'd grown up together. Albie had watched the clumsy, big-footed pup grow into a sleek shepherd that could herd cattle or run down foxes or guard the baby, Alice Anne. Now Shep was gone. Drowned. Like Daisy and Violet and . . . STOP! Think of something else. Think of Alice Anne without the now dead Shep.

Had Albie been asked at any time in his past whom he would miss most if he ever left home, he would, naturally, have said his mother. He could not have predicted it would be Alice Anne.

Elizabeth, a year younger than Albie, could more than take care of herself. She was able to cook and bake breads and cakes, and she could weave a cloth almost as fine and tight as her mother could. Autumn, the mare their father had gotten in a trade from Samuel Abernathy a year ago, would not permit Albie to get his foot near a stirrup. Albie's father could saddle her only after lengthy contests of will and strength. She was as docile as a lamb for Elizabeth, who, if she wished, could ride without a saddle.

Alice Anne, six years old, stayed at Albie's heels. He always protested her presence, but when she wasn't there, he went out of his way to attract her. When he accompanied his father on hunting or fishing or trapping expeditions, he always returned with special treasures for Alice Anne: a flat rock with the fossil imprint of a bone or a leaf, a bleached skull of a bird, a set of antlers, pussy willows, pods of wild grapes, feathers from hawks or owls or pheasants or eagles. It was Albie who'd taught Alice Anne how to milk a cow, who'd shown her where, in tall grass, hens were likely to hide their eggs. Last year, for Christmas, he'd given her a life-size pony he'd carved and fitted together from select pieces of fir. His father had helped him bend the rockers, but he'd done everything else alone. For the mane and the tail he'd used real horsehair, fitting and tying long strands through holes he'd bored along the neck and on the rump. He'd carved the saddle and fitted a pillow to it and covered it with deerhide. From the wooden belly he'd hung old stirrups he'd found in a dilapidated shack in the hills. In the two months since Christmas he'd already replaced the pillow twice.

Would he ever see Alice Anne again?

The spotted goat, lonely, came in the darkness to where Albie lay. Its muzzle prodded Albie's arm, hoping to get its head scratched, but Albie, forcing himself to be strong, turned his back to the animal and locked his hands at his chest. Tomorrow or the next day, you stupid goat, you'll be gone. Eaten. Slaughtered and eaten. You stupid goat.

When the goat gave up and lay down in the middle of the room, Albie rolled onto his back again, trying to locate the rectangular window. Impossible. There was not the slightest variation of black in the entire room. He might as well keep his eyes closed.

With his eyes closed, Albie wondered where all the sounds were coming from. What caused them? What, for example, caused such a contrast between the sound of the rain striking the glass and the rain striking the exterior of the house? Why was it raining so much? Why didn't it stop? Would it rain forever? And the wind, would it never die down? Where was the sun? Would

64

there never again be sunlight? How far had he traveled? Was he still floating down the Mississippi or was he in the Gulf? Or the Atlantic Ocean? Could the world be coming to an end?

Why spend time on such questions? He was not able to answer them and, even if he could, what good would answers do him? Would answers save him? Return him to his mother and his father and his sisters? No. Then what could he do? He could hang on as long as he could and then . . . well, whatever was to happen would happen.

Albie shot up through the ceiling of his sleep like a fish breaking the surface of a lake. Under the blanket his hands were pressing down on his chest. What was it? What had he heard? Could someone be out there in the darkness? He sat up. There. There it was again. A low grunt of a cough, a wheezing cough.

He left his bed and went to the doorway. A low grunting, wheezing cough. But it was more than a grunt. It was almost a cry of pain, of painful exertion. Was the lion dying? Was he choking on one of the bones from that unfortunate white goat?

Albie listened, standing in one position so long that his legs began to tremble. The sound came once more and then did not come again. He returned through the darkness to his bed and again drew the blanket over his body. He ought to sleep in the closet. But that was impossible. There was not room enough there to even sit. He'd be a prisoner in a cage more wretched than the lion's cage.

It didn't matter. Nothing mattered. He was exhausted, defeated. Let the lion come in. Let him finish the whole thing right now. Albie groaned, every joint and every muscle aching with the anticipation of everything coming to an end. He'd not eaten and he wouldn't eat, he'd never see Alice Anne again, and the world was certainly coming to an end. In the half-collapsed bed he waited, inert, uncaring, no longer even wanting to groan, no longer needing or wanting to scream back at the drum-drum-drumming rain, the whistling wind, that despicable river that would be lapping at the side of the house through eternity. He could not even cry.

Eyes closed, he prayed that whenever it came, death should be instantaneous. No lingering pain, no hovering fear. Let the lion, when he decided to strike, accomplish his mission fast, as he had with the white goat. One quick, mighty, final blow.

How long he'd been staring at the window before he realized that it was filled with daylight, he didn't know.

The rain had stopped.

Albie threw the blankets aside. He opened the window and leaned out. Yes, it had stopped raining. His eyes swept the vast sea that was, it seemed, not quite so brown, not scattered with quite so much debris. The horizon was obscured by heavy banks of fog, but he searched the edges of the fog and, in narrower circles, the entire stretch of water between horizon and house. There was only the water, only the debris.

The spotted goat, its legs tucked under, was watching him, waiting for its breakfast. Albie swallowed and closed his eyes. He'd have to clean the room today. The goats had fouled so much of the floor that the odor made his already uneasy stomach shrink and rebel. He left his room and walked down the hallway. The lion was still stretched out in his cage, either asleep or dead.

Albie felt safer, sure that a sick lion was less likely to attack him. He worked steadily, taking no precautions to be quiet. Using the wooden column he'd used before, he pried and slid the bed that was holding the door open. When the bed was at the point where one more thrust would free the door, Albie stopped and looked back. The lion's head was up, his amber eyes half closed, his mouth open. He was panting. As exhuasted or as sick as he was, the cat managed a quiet but surly growl.

Yes, the lion was sick. It had to have been the goat. Or those branches he'd been chewing. The opening in the branches, Albie noticed, was now almost large enough for the lion to push through. Another hour or two would have done it. Well, perhaps he'd be dead before he could enjoy his freedom. Perhaps Albie's precautionary work wasn't really necessary.

Why was he again feeling sorry for the lion? Because, he decided, the animal's about to die. But he'd seen other animals die and he'd never felt especially sorry for them. He'd killed several deer, helped kill pigs and bulls, and, once, had been in on the killing of a grizzly. Why, then, should he be so stricken now? He knew. He needed, desperately needed, not just another live animal in this house with him, but a live animal that could also fight to survive. As long as this lion breathed and lived, he could draw from its strength and will a strength and will of his own. He had no choice but to keep the animal alive. It *had* to live.

Would the lion drink some water? He'd not had any water since he'd been hurled into the house with that tree.

In his room Albie selected a pot he'd brought from the kitchen. He went to the end of the hallway, stepped through the hole where the window had been and onto one of the heavy branches. He walked down the branch to the water and filled the pot.

He straightened, started back into the house, and stopped. This was the first time he'd been outside. He leaned against a limb and looked at the house, evaluating the damage. Were it not for the tree, which was supporting the house, every wall would probably be collapsed by now. Luck had been with him. The tree had saved the house, and then the same tree, caging the lion, had saved him.

His mother would refer to ten or fifteen pages of Scripture to prove that God's eye had been upon him from the very first. His father, not with the same firm conviction but with his own private brand of certainty, would agree. The family had rarely traveled into town to go to church, but when they had, the fervor of the preparations, and the pleasure and relief that lasted long after, had more than made up for their infrequent attendance. The Bible had been read at least twenty minutes every evening, either by his mother or his father. Standing on that branch, admitting it was not just *chance* that had saved him, Albie raised his eyes to the sky. Would the same God who had protected him now continue His protection, prove His benevolence, and send a man and not a tree to take him home? Tonight he'd pray. It could do no harm.

Albie carried the water back to the lion's room. He stepped closer to the cage. If the lion didn't move, he could slip the pot under the bottom branch, near the head. The lion, lying partially on his stomach and partially on his side, had his head turned away. Was he already dead?

Albie set the pot on the floor. He was close enough to hear the heavy, strained breathing, to see bits of tissue and fresh blood on the floor. The lion was bleeding. It had to be the lion. The goat's blood would not be fresh. Albie reached out to stroke the beautiful yellow-brown neck, to offer the lion, in the last moments of his life, some sense of peace. How forlorn, how weak and vulnerable he looked now!

His hand hovered above the tawny neck. There, around the neck, almost covered by the fur, was a leather belt as wide as Albie's wrist, and, hanging from the belt, a piece of rope eight or ten inches long. Both the belt and the rope were worn and scarred. Where the belt had been slashed by thorns or chewed, perhaps, by other animals (his mate? his mates?), the leather was almost torn through.

The lion had been held captive by someone. By whom? How long? The fragment of rope was too old and too frayed for Albie to know if it had been torn or chewed or cut.

So the lion, free, had been captured and freed and once again captured.

"Poor lion," Albie said, and he looked about him to see who had spoken the words. He was more surprised than embarrassed when he realized the words had come from him. Poor lion, indeed. If the lion had lived and escaped from the cage, it would have been *poor Albie*. Even so, he said, "Poor lion," once more when the lion sought to raise his head, to cough. The cough caught in his throat and came out as a series of gasps. His ribs heaved, and one front paw came up, weakly, to try to reach the belt. The paw, limp, dropped to the floor.

Had he not shifted to his knees and, in shifting, bent forward, Albie probably would not have noticed the fragment of branch caught beneath the belt. It could only have broken from one of the limbs the lion had been chewing. Caught under the collar that had already been tight, that extra tension was now choking the lion to death—or possibly had already choked it to death.

Albie raced to his room, grabbed the scissors from his mother's sewing box, and ran back, to kneel behind the lion, to fit the scissors under the belt. The scissors barely made an indentation on the thick leather. He struggled to find a worn area, located one, sawed at it with the edge of the blade until, with a soft click, the collar separated. Albie rubbed the lion's neck, his throat and his chest. The hoarse breathing returned, the hoarseness disappeared. The lion coughed, groaned, shook his head, tried to rise, fell back, then lifted his head again and coughed again.

Albie slid the pot of water forward. The lion, with a snarl and a spit that sent Albie backward as if it had been a fist striking a heavy blow, leaped to his feet and dropped from his stomach, where they'd been suckling, two still wet, still bloody, spotted cubs.

Running to the bed, crawling over it, pushing it forward, slamming the door closed, Albie leaned back and shook his head, trying to remember, trying to believe what he had seen.

He moved about in his room without plan, in a daze. He performed one act after another without thinking about what he was doing. Then he stopped. He knew, suddenly, what he was doing, what he had to do.

He pulled every drawer from the heavy oak dresser and ran down the hall to retrieve the column he'd used as a pry. Back in his room, he pushed and tugged and pried the dresser across the room. It had taken Sam Abernathy and his father an hour to move the dresser up the stairs and now Albie was moving it alone. He rested for a moment in the hall and then moved it again, tugging and prying the piece up the hall toward the hole through which, a few minutes ago, he'd gone to get water for what he'd believed was a dying lion. A dying *he* lion!

Once the dresser was against the wall and, except for a space of about twelve inches at the top, covering the hole, Albie ran back and forth, from his room to the dresser, returning the drawers so the dresser would be heavier and more difficult to move.

Albie returned to his room and sat at the window.

The goat came to him and dropped its chin in his lap. Without realizing what he was doing, he absently stroked the head and scratched the base of each ear.

A *mother* lion with two babies.

He recalled his father's warning that day they'd trailed the lion that had killed Rose, their milk cow. "Now remember, Albie. The closest thing to hell on earth is coming round a bend and finding yourself face to face with a mother cougar and her babies. You do that, you better have six men with you with two rifles for each man. And a pack of twenty good cougar hounds."

The goat snuggled deeper and then leaped back, its body twitching as if twenty wires were pulling it twenty different directions. Albie ran for the closet.

He stood at the door, ready to leap inside. Chills crackled up and down his spine as the lion snarled and growled and scratched at the door of her room. She was free.

CHAPTER 5

The lion's claws tore at the door. Her grunts and
snarls seemed to be in this room, in Albie's ears, inside
his body. She was sure to discover the hole in the wall
torn by the thrust of the tree limbs. She'd crawl down
the tree and, seeing the opening above the dresser, she'd
try to enter. But the opening, Albie was sure, was too
high and too small. She'd have no footing for her hind
feet, and the surface her front claws would try to grip,
the top of the dresser, had been polished to a high gloss.
She'd not be able to move it.

He'd be wise, just in case, to have a weapon. Was there anything better than the scissors, which he kept close at all times now? One more search downstairs might turn something up. His rifle was under the water, on the floor. It would be useless until he cleaned and dried every tiny working piece, but he could do it. But then what? What good was a rifle without ammunition?

There would be table knives. Cleavers. And, as the Indians had done, he could fashion slivers of boards into spears. The silver table knife could shape the ends into points sharp enough to pierce the lion's body. With two or three such spears he might be able to hold the lion at bay if she were to get past that barricade. He could do it. The Indians had. So had the gladiators. The history book his mother had carried with her ever since she'd been a child contained a print he used to study in front of the fire. Chin in hands, eyes half closed, he'd be carried by the flames into the arena, at the side of the gladiator wearing a brief skirt and blouse of scaled metal. Together they faced not one but two lions emerging from the pit in the background. Like his comrade, he held in his right hand a single, thin, heavy-headed spear and in his left a long, thin dagger. The crowd in the curved amphitheater cheered the lions while the Emperor, Nero, sulked in his chair, bored, eyes hooded and chin in hand.

As the intensity and volume of the scratches and growls increased, the goat strained at its tether, bleating for Albie to come to its rescue as he'd come once before. He refused to be tricked by compassion now. He

74

walked past the goat with hands held high, so he'd not yield to any temptations to pet the animal. Again to distract it rather than to appease its hunger, Albie emptied a jar of beans at the goat's feet.

He paused at the closed door of the lion's room. There was nothing to imply her presence on the other side of the door. No scratching, no growling. Perhaps, too concerned about her new cubs to wander very far from them, she'd not leave the room for the next few days. In that time Albie might be rescued. If he weren't rescued . . . well, now was the time.

At the landing Albie removed his clothes. He gasped and groaned as the water climbed his body. He pushed free of the stairs and floated, trying to examine the surface of the water as he kicked his legs and paddled his arms. He could not stay in the water too long. It was cold, and his arms and legs were beginning to ache. He selected five long pieces of wood, all of them, he suspected, from studs or beams or wallboards. After taking them up the steps and onto the landing, he returned to the water. He paddled to the broken hulk of what had been the stone chimney, held a deep breath, and let his body sink. Clutching at the few remaining rough stones forming the face of the chimney, he pulled himself lower and lower. When he reached the thick oak slab that had rested above the hearth, Albie had to turn and fight his way back toward the surface. Stars exploded behind his eyes, and a fire burned in his lungs. When he thought he could hold his breath no longer but must open his mouth, must suck in the muddy water, he broke through, into the air.

Clinging desperately to one of the shelves in the open closet, Albie waited until his strength returned, until the fire died down in his chest and his breathing returned to normal.

After several deep breaths he closed his eyes and lowered himself again, working his way down the fragmented chimney face until he reached the oak slab. Pieces of the hearth were still intact. There had been four hooks imbedded in the stone. Tongs, pokers, and log-clamps had hung from these hooks. They were gone now. All except one poker. Albie removed it from its hook.

With the fire once again in his lungs, the stars again exploding behind his eyes, he stroked and kicked, moving up. Up, up, up. Again, just as it seemed he'd not be able to hold his breath a moment longer, he broke free. He rested once more at the cupboard and then paddled to the steps. He climbed the stairs and laid the poker alongside the wooden strips soon to be shaped into spear shafts.

He draped some clothes around his body, and he sat on the landing, his feet on the third step, one step above the water. He listened for sounds of the lion, but she was no longer struggling at the door. Everything was quiet.

Sitting there, regaining his strength, Albie worked to re-create the image of the kitchen, so he might more easily search out clues that could lead him to drawers or cupboards, hidden or rarely-thought-of niches where he might find something he could use as a weapon. What had each of the many drawers contained? How had the furniture in the kitchen been arranged?

Strange. He'd taken it all for granted. He'd never stopped to see just what was where. Now he had to concentrate to re-create it all. Against the wall, across the room, opposite the fireplace, had been the whatnot, its shelves filled with china and crockery. Not the dishes used every day, but the special dishes that were brought out when, for instance, the Abernathys traveled on a Sunday afternoon in the summer for a visit that always ended with their staying for dinner. Very special glasses and crocks and bowls used, for instance, the night that salesman from Duluth had stayed over, the night he'd described that exotic, faraway world of the Mississippi steamboat. "Very attractive china," he'd said. "Are the glasses from Boston, perhaps. From . . . ?" and he'd named a very expensive shop that Albie's mother had heard about when she'd been a child. "Just something my grandmother passed on to us," his mother had replied, solemn but unable to disguise her pleasure.

All those glasses were gone now. Lost forever. And the whatnot? Also gone. But wouldn't it be floating if it had fallen over? It wasn't in the room, which meant that it had been sucked through one of the ruptures in the walls. But none of the ruptures were large enough to permit such a large piece of furniture to float through. It must have sunk. The weight of its contents, held securely behind locked doors, had carried it under, down through the water to the floor.

What had been to the left of the whatnot? The two

storage cupboards, one filled with bags of dried beans and nuts and potatoes and boxes and cans of other foods. Those cupboards were empty now. The table! Between the hearth and the wall, in the center of the room: the table, with the carefully latched drawer containing cleavers and carving knives. Cleavers! Knives! In the drawer of that table floating now, upside down, near the hole next to the door. The few boards between the hole and the door could be torn away at any moment, creating a space large enough for table, whatnot, cupboards and all to flow through.

He had to try once more.

Albie entered the water with a leap and paddled to the table, which was floating with its legs out of the water. Holding to a strip of exposed stud with his right hand, Albie moved his left hand down the leg of the table to the smooth top. The drawer was on the other side. He eased the table about and felt again for the drawer. It was gone. The tips of his fingers traced the opening. The drawer, which had been designed with a complicated locking device, so Alice Anne could not get to the knives, must have been open. He must have left it open himself. Well, it was gone. It had probably fallen out when the table had been upended.

Albie clutched at the stud with both hands. He could not dive down again. Even if the knives and cleavers were lying there on the floor, he could not do it. But he had to—just once more if he wanted to live to be rescued so he might return home, so he might live again with his mother and father and Elizabeth and Al . . .

Holding the fourth deep breath, Albie threw himself forward, upturning his body so his head was down. His previous efforts had gained him a certain assurance, so he moved faster and more easily now, his right hand always in touch with the wall, touching for guidance as well as security. The wall, having been built by his grandfather, offered that old reassurance that had always been generated by the stories his father had told about the old man. It was as if his grandfather were diving with him now, urging him on, reminding him that he came of sturdy and honorable stock, that he had no choice but to respect that ancestry.

Albie tried once to open his eyes, but the water was so thick with silt and debris that he felt as if he were opening his eyes in a sandstorm. He closed his eyes tightly and pulled himself down. His head was down and his arms forward. Suddenly there was no wall for his right hand to feel, to hold to.

The floor of the house was gone.

Another few inches and he would be under the house, with the house floating over him, passing him by. For a moment he thought that had already happened. He tumbled about in the water and swam toward the surface as fast, as strenuously, as he could. His left hand brushed a board. It was the wall. He was still inside the house. But he could just as well be outside, touching an exterior wall. A scream tried to free itself from his throat as he fought his way upward. He wanted to stop stroking with his arms so his hands might be free to tear the fire from his lungs. He continued, though, holding his breath, stroking, kicking. When he did break through the surface, when he did wipe the grit from his eyes, when he observed the walls all about him, he did scream.

Albie held the stud again until he could hand-walk his way around the interior. When he reached the stairs and was able to climb, he ignored the material he'd deposited on the landing and went into his room, no longer taking special care to be quiet, not stopping to determine the presence or the significance of sounds in the lion's room. He wrapped himself in a blanket from the bed. When he stopped shivering, he returned to the landing and dressed. He brought the boards and the poker to his room.

The shortest piece of wood, he decided, after examining all five pieces, could make a dagger. The others, though they'd have to be shaped and sharpened, could be spears.

He felt better now. He was working to save himself, or at least to keep himself alive until others could save him. He acknowledged a newer, deeper respect for his grandfather, who'd fought off Indians and wolves and marched west, and then farther west, three times, building and leaving homes and homesteads each time. With only an ax and a flintlock, and a heart harder than the iron ax blade. His grandfather, if he were alive, would be proud of his grandson.

Albie chose a pint of venison and opened the lid without exertion. He felt as if in the last single hour he'd grown from boy to man. He ate all the meat and drank the juice and was sure he could feel the strength seeping into his veins.

He took up the short piece of wood and tried to cut it with the silver table knife. The watersoaked wood repelled the blade. There was barely a depression on the sheath of the wood after five minutes of carving.

He selected one of the long pieces, thinking it might respond differently. It didn't. His fingers ached, the palm of his right hand was swollen and pink, and two large blisters bloomed on his thumb and forefinger.

Albie threw the wood aside.

While he'd been working, the goat had been trying to outreach its tether, to nip his thigh or lay its head in his lap. To keep it from bleating and arousing the lion, Albie opened a jar of corn. He drank the juice, took a mouthful of the grains, and poured the rest on the floor. The goat began chewing, but with the second or third bite both the goat and Albie stiffened.

The coughing scream of the lion seemed to have come from inside the room. Albie found himself in the closet without remembering his having rushed there. The lion, he decided, was not inside the house. She was outside, at the hallway window, scratching at the dresser. Not just scratching at it but throwing herself against it. Scratching and throwing herself and screaming.

She's hungry. And she smells the goat. Oh God, she's hungry.

From the doorway of his room, Albie saw the dresser had been moved two or three inches from the wall. The lion's front paws, at the top of the dresser, were inside the opening, fighting the polished surface for a grip that might help it break down the barrier. She continued hurling herself, hurling, screaming, scratching.

81

The dresser moved another inch or two. As Albie watched, unable, unwilling, to move, he saw the muzzle, the white mouth, there in the opening near the floor. After another scream and another leap, more than just her muzzle was visible. There, for one moment, were a pair of amber eyes stretched to slits by the squeeze of the head in the small opening. The sight of Albie drove the lion into a frenzy. She spit and snarled and clawed more ferociously at the opening, her struggle forcing the dresser another inch from the wall.

Albie turned, searching frantically for his only weapon, the scissors. The goat, stiff-legged, quivering, was too terrified to do anything more than roll its eyes and deposit a mound of excrement. It did not even think now to pull at its tether.

Albie kneeled and hugged the foul-smelling goat in his arms. He kissed its muzzle and hugged it again. "I'm sorry," he said.

He hurried the animal into the hallway and tied it to the leg of the dresser as the lion's head, the entire head, thrust itself through the opening. She saw the goat and smelled it and twisted and turned with such an explosion of energy that the dresser moved several more inches. Her rear claws were digging into the tree trunk, finding extra leverage. When the dresser moved again, Albie gave the paralyzed goat one final pat on the head and turned and ran into his room. Inside the closet, he closed the door and huddled in the darkness.

A shrill bleat from the goat was stopped abruptly. Albie waited, how long he didn't know, but when he opened the door, just a crack, he saw the rear portion of the lion, rump up high, haunches tucked under, the long brown tail straight out with its black tip twitching. A stream of blood appeared, moved slowly down the floorboards. The lion backed up, to capture the dark fluid. Albie heard the rough sandpaper tongue tearing at the wood. Then, and in full view now, the lion turned to peer inside the room. She stared directly at the closet. Albie drew the door closed and held it as tightly as his weak fingers could manage.

He counted to a hundred, twice, and he concentrated on the spots on the interior lids of his closed eyes. When he looked again, the lion was still there, a bright red chunk of some organ hanging from her jaws.

When he was unable to endure the strain any longer, Albie relaxed his arms and his back and neck. If he didn't sit soon, he'd collapse. His legs were rubbery, and his entire spine, from his hips to the base of his skull, was one long, thumping pain. He opened the door enough to see the lion in the doorway, stretched out, licking her front paws. She looked like a peaceful, giant kitten—and sounded like one. Albie could hear her rumbling purr.

Slowly, very slowly, Albie's legs buckled. The door flew open, and he fell forward. He tried to stand, to run, but his legs refused to obey his command. He tried to slide his hands under his chest, to lift himself, but his arms would not function.

When he'd tumbled out of the closet, the lion had leaped erect, spitting. Albie lay still, his back to the lion, hearing the low growl.

She's coming. Now. He closed his eyes and held his breath.

When nothing happened, he rolled his head onto his left cheek. The lion was lying flat, stretched out, purring again, licking her right paw. She seemed no more interested in Albie's presence than she was in the sound of the rain, which came with a sudden steady downpour.

Albie changed his position, drawing his legs forward, sitting up, turning, easing ever so slightly, ever so slowly, back toward the closet. Was he delirious? Had the loneliness, the fear, the desperation, driven him out of his mind? Was he dead already and drifting in the land of the spirit? Had death been so swift that he'd suffered no pain?

He tried to move his arm, to locate the closet door, but his arm seemed empty of bone, free of muscle. He fell back again onto his side. The lion jerked, spit quietly and briefly, and then returned to the cleaning of her paws. She paused, glanced at Albie, and began washing her face. She interrupted herself to glance at Albie again.

Albie stopped moving. He heard a chirping, almost birdlike whistle several times before he sensed the sound was coming from her. She rolled, still offering her birdlike chirp, onto her back. She lay quietly, her front paws curled, then she rolled onto her side, her back to Albie. With a loud grunt and again those gentle, chirping sounds, she rolled once more to face him. The flesh surrounding her protruding nipples was covered with tiny red scratches. She stood and moved toward him.
Now!

Albie closed his eyes. *Alice Anne . . . Alice Anne . . . good-bye . . .*

When he opened his eyes, he saw the lion stretched out on her stomach, her front paws beyond her nose, her head erect, her long tail straight out behind her. She could have reached out her paw and touched Albie. But she didn't. Watching him through sleepy eyes, she continued purring.

He'd endured too much. Simply, smoothly, abruptly, Albie relaxed and lost consciousness. When he awakened, he heard the rain striking the window, and he heard the wind creeping across the roof. It was almost dark. He raised his head. He was alone in the room.

CHAPTER 6

Up from the floor and on the bed, angry at the dusty darkness once again sifting over the house . . . over the water and over the world . . . hating those now intimate twin enemies, the wind and the rain, Albie tried to calculate the number of nights he'd been afloat. But he could not think of multiple *nights*, he could only think of one night, one single night that refused to be cut into single sheets of separate nights.

Albie left the bed and went to the window. The same

dreary scene: the endless, undulating brown meadow of water. In the deep dusk, like an angry victim deciding he'd submitted to attacks too long, it was striking back at the vicious darts of rain.

Back in bed and finally asleep, he pleaded with the desperate faces of the goats to stop chasing each other through his dream. They did interrupt their chase to appeal for protection. In unison they bleated their protest at his betrayal. He leaped up, awake, shouting his defense aloud. "I had to . . . I had to . . . I have to get home . . . I want to see Alice Anne. . ."

Shivering in the darkness, Albie listened for the faintest suggestion of sound to warn him that the mountain lion had entered the room. Satisfied that she'd not, he settled again under his blankets.

As he settled and drifted again into sleep, a great hand dipped down, scooped him up, lifted him gently, and then dumped him hard on the floor. He climbed to his feet, thinking that this had been the first time he'd ever walked in his sleep. A new sensation pressed up through each foot. It was not so much the presence of a new sensation as the absence of the old one. A force was tugging at the house. And, in its efforts to resist, every board in the house seemed to strain and squeal. For a moment the two of them, Albie and the house, seemed to be traveling in different directions, but then, and again it was sudden, the old sensations were there on the floorboards.

Back on the bed, under the blankets, Albie considered the phenomenon, the push and then the pull and then the sense of drift. Had the tree, with the house in its branches, gone over a waterfall? Had there been a collision with another tree? A bridge? Another boat? If there'd been a boat, he would have heard voices.

Whatever it had been, it was lost.

In the morning, with the rain splashing against the gray window, Albie had no desire to leave his bed and search for boats. He closed his eyes. He'd sleep for a few more minutes. Why shouldn't he if he wanted to? He wasn't going out of this house. He had no chores to do. The lion would be satisfied for another day or two. And perhaps, during the day, another barn or pen would float into range, to provide a few chickens or a sheep or even another goat.

Where was the lion? Was she staying away because of her cubs? Albie sat up. Had something happened to her? During the night, that bump . . . had she been hurt?

Albie looked about the room, trying to find some evidence that would explain the strange event of the night before, but he found only the deposits of the goats. The odor was growing stronger. He had to clean the room, but before he did, he had to know if the lion had been injured or killed.

Killed? Fearing an investigation might prove her death, he was even more reluctant to get out of bed, to force himself to investigate. If she *were* dead, he'd once again be alone in this house on this river-ocean. Even if she were alive and tomorrow betrayed the conditions of her own truce, she would be *alive*, a reflection of his own, of Albie's, aliveness. If she were dead, those sealed amber eyes would be an omen of his own impending death, a guarantee that all hope for a rescue would be useless. He had to know.

Sliding out from under the blankets, he sat, apprehensive, on the edge of the bed, and then he pushed himself toward the door.

The hall, cautiously inspected, proved to be empty. The water, he noticed, was no longer running like a creek along the hallway, but the floor, open to sheets of rain swept in through the broken wall, was still soaked. Had that creek still been running, it might have washed away the remnant of hair he had to step over, the discarded bones, the spot of dark blood.

Why *wasn't* the water running? The rain was still falling—he knew that too well. Had the wind reversed its direction? Had the river started to drop?

And the lion, had it leaped into the water, thinking it safe now, after a cow or horse it had seen? Some lions, he knew, if they'd been raised near water, could swim long distances. He and his father had once followed the trail of a cougar that had dragged the corpse of a calf in its jaws for nearly half a mile. The trail had led across the Redman River. But the width of the Mississippi was fifty, maybe a hundred times that of the Redman. And compared to this boiling, humming current, the flow of the Redman was as gentle as the surface of a pond.

Had that stupid lion panicked and deserted her cubs? Had she left them for *him* to care for? Damn her! Where were those instincts wild animals and Indians, according to his father, just naturally possessed? Safe

90

now, in a forest, she'd suffer remorse for a few days, but then she'd continue her life as if she'd never had those cubs.

At the end of the hallway, the closet he'd intended to serve as a barrier had fallen against the wall. It lay on one side, angled across the opening, its legs at the baseboard on the right and its top against the wall on the left, near the ceiling trim. Supporting himself on the closet, Albie leaned forward. The wind hurled the rain at his face with such intensity that he had to squint. He saw why he'd been lifted and thrown from his bed last night.

Several trees as large or larger than the tree that had been his host these past few days had joined other trees which, days or weeks, or perhaps even months, before the flood, had caught on an underwater snag. Together, they formed a network of limbs and branches, many of them below the water's surface. This network, which had caught and held his tree, was already catching additional trees, shrubs, bits and pieces of logs and lumber, and derelict portions of farm buildings. His house was no longer floating down the river.

The water, though, was flowing—flowing past, around, under, and through the island of logs and trees. The island, even as Albie observed it, was expanding inch by inch, bush by bush, board by board. Soon another tree would join this one, and then another would join it. In less than a week, if the flood did not let up, the island would be twice the size it was now.

If the house were in the ocean, or even in the Gulf, it

would not be stopped like this. That meant he was still on the river. So his luck was improving. The longer the house remained here, trapped, not moving, the better were his chances for rescue. When the storm stopped, and it *had* to stop eventually, and the water began to recede, the island would probably have to be destroyed so it would not be a hazard to river navigation. When they came to destroy it, he'd be found.

Feeling better, and even relieved of the anger he'd felt for the lion, Albie stepped over the angled dresser and through the opening onto the tree trunk. He half closed his eyes against the rain and picked his way along the trunk, dropping occasionally to his hands and knees when the mossy bark grew slippery. He didn't want to fall into that growling, hissing brown foam and float into the web of limbs and branches that could trap him and, with a shift or roll, dash him under the surface.

The secondary limb, the one that had speared its way through the wall of his parents' room, sloped up into the house. Albie crept forward, to the broken wall. He lifted one leg and was about to pull in the other when the air was split by a scream. The scream had come from the only sheltered portion of the room, the closet.

Near the entry to the closet lay a pile of matted fur and horns. Suspended above the remnants of the goats, the great tawny head seemed larger and more menacing than it had before.

As she recognized Albie, the lion seemed (so it appeared to Albie) to relax. Or had it been his imagination? Wistful, wishful thinking? A low growl was continuing to rumble in the lion's throat, but when she blinked her eyes, they dropped their gleam, to grow soft and lustrous, and the growl disappeared inside a heavy, rhythmic purr. As if she realized her mistake, she returned to work on the ragged remains of what appeared to be a thigh bone.

The fur of both of her forelegs and her white muzzle were smeared with blood. She brought up her head to sweep her long white whiskers, white under the blood, with her thick red-brown tongue. She looked directly at Albie and chirped. When he withdrew his leg and started to leave, she again, and again with a regal nonchalance, returned to her meal.

Not only was the lion safe, and not stupid, she'd been wise enough to take advantage of the only sheltered space in the room, as close an approximation to a cave as she could find. Albie's final glance took his breath away, and, hunched down on hands and knees, with the rain running down his collar, he chuckled. That blood-smeared, open-mouthed grin, that regal and independent and authoritative thrust of the head, hurled him back home to the face of Alice Anne. He caught himself laughing at her jelly-smeared face, shaking his head at her contemptuous self-reliance. "Well," Albie said, and he chuckled again as the lion rocked her head at the strange sounds coming from the boy's mouth. "Well, if we're gonna be together, you better have a name. I can't just call you *lion*. And there is only one other name. You sure are an Alice, I'll tell you." Albie laughed, and the lion's neck stretched out, and again the head rocked from shoulder to shoulder and her purring and her chirping stopped, as if the sound of laughter were somehow familiar, familiar and reassuring.

Albie backed out of the room, murmuring, "Alice . . . you're just like Alice."

In his mother's workroom, in the shattered drawer of a shattered cabinet, he found a small brush he'd often seen his mother use to whisk the lint and loose threads from a piece of cloth she was working on.

He collected the broken fragments of glass in his room, the empty jars, the lids, the red rubber washers, and the dung, and he dropped everything out of the window, into the water. Using the small brush, he collected the smaller bits of glass and remnants of dung. A rag, held outside the window, was soaked in a few seconds. After several minutes of scrubbing, Albie had succeeded in turning the dark brown stains to gray. There was enough left of the large stain in the hall to remind him, every time he'd be stepping over it, of the dumb trust that goat had offered him. Why, after having witnessed so many animals slaughtered, cows and pigs and rabbits and goats and chickens and turkeys and pheasants and grouse, why should he be so stricken now at the death of two more beasts? He had to keep reminding himself that the death of the goats had been necessary. More necessary, in fact, than all those other killings he'd participated in.

After the room was in order, Albie sat by the window. He dozed and awakened and dozed until it was almost dark. He decided he was hungry. That was why he was being distracted by those strange sounds

94

which, he knew now, had to be grumblings and growlings in his stomach.

A pint jar of rabbit meat and a pint jar of peaches satisfied both his hunger and his thirst. He felt more secure, more optimistic, than he had any night since the house had been carried off by the flood. Something good would happen—it had to. He'd not been saved just to be killed. God wouldn't . . . and at the thought of God he remembered that he had promised himself that he would pray. He hadn't. All right, he'd keep his promise. But he had to be precise. He didn't want to irritate God, asking for just any favor. He'd simply ask for deliverance. And while he was asking for his deliverance, why not (wasn't the lion one of God's creatures, too?) why not ask for the deliverance of the lion? Of that jelly-faced lion named Alice.

Should he actually *pray* for a dumb beast? Wouldn't that offend God? Ah, but how often his mother had assured him that *His eye is on the sparrow*. How appropriate that he should recall her words now. If His eye is on the sparrow, His eye will surely be on the lion.

Albie removed his damp clothes, dried himself, and dressed. He knelt at the side of the bed and closed his eyes and folded his hands as he had folded them so many times before.

Be brief, his mother had always advised him. God had millions of other prayers to hear and respond to, so it would be ungracious to waste His time with ramblings. "God, please save me and Alice, the lion, and her babies."

Was that brief enough? Should he suggest terms? Or

should he leave the technique to God? No, that was enough. If He had His eye on the sparrow and the lion and Albie, He also had His ear tuned. He'd heard and He'd know what to do.

Albie curled up under the blankets, thinking about the cubs and how snug they must be, curled within that warm fur. He snuggled with them, pushing his face into that warm, furry belly. But the goats stomped their feet, demanding his attention. The white one and then the spotted one: they marched before him, urging on another pair, one white and one spotted. On and on they came, an endless procession of white goats and spotted goats, their faces drawn into fierce scowls of protest, of denunciation, in pairs, heads bobbing, all of them bleating their sad, solemn chorus.

Then, instead of bleating, they were talking— talking as people talk, calling to him. "Hey," they shouted, "anyone in there? Anyone in that house?"

Albie pushed his way through the goats, through the furry faces and bleating voices.

Daylight. Bright sunlight.

The rain, and the wind, had stopped.

"Hello . . . anyone in there?"

Running before he was free of the blankets, Albie fell and leaped up and kicked his way to the window.

A boat, about two hundred yards away, was moving toward him, moving closer, its two paddle wheels revolving slowly. A squat black stack continued to pour thick black smoke after the boat stopped about a hundred yards from the tangled mass of trees.

Delta Belle.

The name, in chipped and faded gray script, stretched across the side.

A glorious pure-white boat.

At the railing two bearded men were peering through cupped hands in Albie's direction. Albie waved, tried several times to call, but could only manage a few cracked clearings of his throat. He looked up at the first sunny sky he had seen in, it seemed, his entire lifetime.

"Anyone . . . hey, Big Rafe, there's a man . . . it's a boy . . . there's a boy in that house . . ."

CHAPTER 7

"Here . . . I'm over here."

All over. It was all over. He was saved.

Albie's patience, his faith, his refusal to submit to hysteria, had been rewarded. Soon, in a week or two, he'd be back home with his mother and father and Elizabeth and Alice Anne. People would come from miles around to look at him and show him off to the kids, and there'd probably even be stories about him in some newspaper. He wouldn't have to go to bed before his mother and father any more; he would stay up as late as he wanted. He'd be invited to places to tell people his story.

Would anyone believe him?

Well, given such a chance, what normal boy, they'd say, with winks at each other, what normal boy would be so simple-minded to tell the ordinary, unvarnished truth? Exaggerations are to be expected from fourteen-year-old boys. Fathers and uncles would chuckle and cluck their tongues and mothers and aunts would beam with patient sympathy and understanding, and children would stare and would even say *Gosh* or *Dadgum it*, awed and envious, but all would continue honoring him because he sure enough would have survived the flood. That couldn't be denied, and that, in itself, would be a miracle. No other word for it. But all that hogwash about that lion and her two cubs . . . well, the boy would *have* to be respected for his will to survive, and, yes, even for his ability to tell tall stories at such an early age. But the mere fact of having endured that trip down the Mississippi: that alone was incredible enough to permit any boy to be indulged.

It wouldn't matter. Albie didn't care if they didn't believe him. What was important was his rescue, and *that* was being organized this very minute.

Thanks to that salesman from Duluth that wintery night, Albie knew there were larger, fancier boats than the *Delta Belle*, but now, at this moment, to Albie, the *Delta Belle* was the most beautiful object the hand of any man could ever have created.

As the boat maneuvered a few feet closer, its side

wheels rumbling and throwing the brown Mississippi water, black smoke belching from its stack, it proved itself more than a match for the river, for the flood that had devastated the land. The rattle of her chains sounded above the rumble of the river, and she stopped, finally, about eighty yards upstream—out of range of the island of debris.

Albie could see two men on the deck. They were fine-looking, with full-bearded faces like his father's.

His father. Oh, wouldn't his father be surprised when he walked over the hill and down the dirt road and up the lane to the Abernathys' house? Wouldn't they be astonished! But could they, in their despair, have given up, gone back east?

They'd stay. Albie knew they would stay. How many sons and daughters had his grandmother and grandfather lost in their move west? Five? Six? And *they'd* never turned back.

Albie smiled as he thought about the house his father was probably already building, high up in the hills. Why, he'd be home in time to help build it.

The two men climbed over the railing of the *Delta Belle* into a yawl that was slung over the side. A third man, at the railing, lowered the yawl, with the other two men in it, by manipulating a wheel and winch. The man on the boat shouted something at the men in the yawl, and then, as the yawl sat in the water and one of the two men let the lines loose, the man at the railing cupped his eyes and looked toward the house.

Albie's wave received no response. The man disappeared. "The sun's in his eyes," Albie thought. "He probably couldn't see me." The man appeared again, and Albie waved again, and the man, after shielding his eyes from the sun, turned and disappeared again.

Albie paced back and forth as the two men rowed across the water. He talked to himself, tapped the windowsill, paced, waved at the men, until, finally, there they were, four feet away, two or three feet below the windowsill. One of the men was holding a coil of rope in the air. "Stand back. Fix this to something solid in there."

Albie stepped aside. The rope sailed in, and he picked it up. His hands trembling, he tied the rope around the sideboard of the bed.

"Pull it tight. We're driftin' back."

He loosened the rope and hauled it in, hand over hand, until the man outside called, "Right there. Tie it there."

Albie tied the rope again and straightened up to see, climbing through the window, a huge bearded bear of a man in greasy clothes. After the initial shock, Albie convinced himself the man was as full of grace and heavenly beauty as the most delicate angel, although the low voice sounded much like his father's when his father was angry.

"Step outa the way there," the big man said, puffing and grunting as he hauled the remainder of his body into the room. The second man followed, more agile but no cleaner. And no more impressed with Albie's presence than the big man had been. They both carried rifles.

"You saved me," Albie said, restraining the urge to break into tears, to rush to them and thank them and throw his arms about them and ask them where he was and how long it would take to get back home.

But the two men did not appear to be especially interested in Albie. They did not introduce themselves or ask who he was or where he was from. They climbed over the windowsill and went directly to the cans and jars and boxes he'd saved from the flood waters.

"Lookit here," the smaller man said. He held various jars up to the light and then, turning abruptly on Albie, he said, "You alone?"

"Yes, I was alone when the flood . . ."

"Looks like venison," the big man said. "Open one of them, Frederick. Don't waste time."

Frederick turned the lid easily, sniffed the contents, grinned at his partner, handed him the jar, and opened another jar for himself. They stuffed the meat into their mouths without looking at Albie. "This proves what I always says," the small man mumbled through his food. "City women, they can't do *nothin'* like this. I bet she's a farm woman. Your momma a farm woman, boy?"

"Yes," Albie said. "We live . . ."

The big man, having emptied the jar, and with both cheeks stuffed, hurled the jar toward the open window. It crashed through the glass. "Oops. Missed."

The small man laughed and tossed his own jar, which cleared the opening. "That's the way to do it," he said, wiping his almost black face with his almost black hands and then wiping his hands on his jacket. The smaller man, Frederick, went up the hall. "Gonna look around," he said. The big man, after several grunts and wipes of hands and mouth, spit a few bones onto the floor and tromped them into the wood on his way across the hall. He tried the door to Albie's parents' room, the lion's room, bumping it with his shoulder and then stepping back to ram it.

"There's nothing in there," Albie said. "It's Ma and Pa's old bedroom. The door's swelled shut. And the walls are all crushed in." He tried to keep his voice natural but could not avoid a faint note of anxiety. He recognized it, but he didn't know if the two men had. He also recognized a swelling fear, a disappointment that was growing heavier, more oppressive. The men were not interested in rescuing him. They didn't even seem interested in his presence. He might as well not have been in the room.

The smaller man, Frederick, returned. "Ain't nothin' in there," Frederick said. "I looked in. Branch of the tree's smashed in one wall. Room's empty, all broke up. Nothin' worth anythin' in it. But we're sure gonna take this food, I tells you. Ain't we, Big Rafe?"

For the first time since they came aboard, the big man looked directly at Albie. "Where you from, boy?"

"Wisconsin."

"Wis . . . how long you been driftin'?"

"I don't know. I lost track. Are you gonna take me back with you?"

The two men looked at each other but said nothing. The big man went to the window and looked outside.

"We ain't stayin' here long," he said. "Can't tell when a tree's gonna swing in here and smash that yawl or block us from getting back."

"Your folks keep money in the house?" Frederick asked. "Your mom wear jewelry?"

"No. We never had any money. Ma never wore any jewelry. Never had any."

"These farmhouses," Frederick said, speaking to his friend. "Like I tells you. Hardly worth the trouble. City houses, they got things worth takin'."

The big man left the window and towered over Albie, glaring down at him. "You ain't lyin' about money, are you, boy?" He shook a greasy finger tipped with a chipped and cracked nail under Albie's nose. "Don't lie to me. I can smell a lie." He lifted his head and sniffed, twice. "Now. Any money in this place?"

"No."

"You sure?" And the man bent low, sniffing at Albie's lips. "I'm tellin' you. I can sniff a lie like a hound can sniff a rabbit."

"I'm telling the truth. Are you . . . are you . . . going to take me . . . ?"

The big man went into the hallway, jerking his head at Frederick. "Come on out here a minute."

The two men whispered and murmured in the hallway for several minutes, their words indistinct but their voices suggesting disagreement.

Who were these men? Were they planning to leave him? Were they not going to take him back to their boat? They'd said they'd be taking food. What would

105

he do? If the lion demanded food tonight and there wasn't even canned food to offer . . . ?

The lion. Alice. He'd forgotten her. If they did take him, what would happen to her?

The men had rifles. If he'd let them find her, they would have shot her. Wasn't that what he wanted? Hadn't *he* searched for weapons with which to defend himself against the lion? *He* had meant to kill her. If they did leave him behind, the least they could do was to help him by putting the lion out of her misery, by killing her now, quickly, so she would not die of slow starvation. But if he'd kept them from finding her, he'd kept them from killing her, he'd saved her, so why should he tell them about her now? He wouldn't. The only thing he'd do would be to ask them to leave one of their rifles. Then, if he had to, he'd be able to defend himself.

The two men continued talking, arguing, in the hallway. Albie heard Big Rafe say, "Well, I think it would be worth it, even if we have to keep him that long." Then the two men returned from the hall. "Where's your folks at now?" Big Rafe asked Albie.

Albie shrugged.

"They dead?"

"No."

"Where are they?"

"Home. Back . . . home. In Wisconsin."

The two men exchanged glances, and the smaller man, called Frederick, approached Albie, his face split open with a smile that exposed five or six tobacco-stained teeth in dark red gums. "I bet your folks be glad to get you back home, I bet."

Albie's hopes soared. "Yes. They sure will be. Then you are taking me with you?"

"Sure we are," the big man agreed. "What made you think we wasn't?" And with that, he crawled through the window and dropped into the yawl. He laid down his rifle and said, "Start moving that stuff, Frederick."

The smaller man signaled Albie to help him carry the jars and boxes and cans to the window. Piece by piece everything was dropped to the man below, who stacked it all in a disorderly pile in the center of the yawl.

"Let's go, boy."

Albie crawled through the window, hung by his hands for a moment, and then dropped.

"I'd say she's gone down a foot already," the big man called to Frederick.

The news seemed to make little difference to Frederick, who spent the next ten or fifteen minutes complaining about his always having to row the yawl. The big man, his rifle across his lap, seemed unimpressed by Frederick's complaints that it wasn't fair that *he* always got the worst jobs. It was him, wasn't it, it was him, Frederick, who'd worked out the whole plan. And who, he pointed out, interrupting his rowing and then picking it up again when the boat began to turn and move downstream, who'd known about the *Delta Belle?* Him. Wasn't it? It was. He'd known where she was docked, he'd known how to free her, and it was him who got to Spider. Spider had done all those repairs—he'd be the first to admit the truth when it was the truth—but it had been him, hadn't it, who'd convinced Spider to join them? But look at what was happening. He was rowing the yawl, like always. The least a fair man could do was to share . . .

Albie turned his head for one last look at the house. The outline of the roof was barely visible through the branches of the trees. Several smaller trees and bushes had piled up in front of the house, interweaved with those already there. Poor Alice. What would she do? How would she find food now? Her cubs would die. Then she would die. And he, Albie, would be alive. Maybe he ought to tell the men about the lion. They could shoot her, as he knew they'd be delighted to do. They'd skin her, even as he himself had helped his father to skin two cougars. He couldn't. Not now. She didn't deserve that indignity, to be shot by men who hated her, who'd sell her pelt, who'd probably dump the cubs in a bag and throw them in the river. Or sell them. Owned by some traveling salesman, shown for a few pennies, they, too, would be collared and chained, and probably caged for life. No, he couldn't, he wouldn't do that.

"Look at that," Federick said, finding someone on whom he might displace his anger. "He's cryin'. We ain't got a boy, we got a girl here."

"Wish we did," the big man said. He gazed up at the sky. "I do think she's all over. Here on, it's dryin'-up time. What you cryin' for, girl?"

Albie wiped his eyes. "I ain't crying."

108

Both men roared, enjoying the mix of embarrassment and anger that distorted Albie's face. The big man opened a jar and stuffed half of the contents into his mouth. Frederick continued complaining about the unfair distribution of labor. The big man belched, wiped his face and hands. "Your mother sure is a fine cook. Now it's a shame *she* wasn't carried off in that house 'stead of you."

Albie pushed a fist against his mouth to stifle his torment. Was he being saved? Would he ever see his mother? His father? Elizabeth? Alice Anne? He lay his head in his arms.

"There he goes again," Frederick said. "Look at him. I mean look at *her*."

Albie jerked up his head and shouted, with all the fury he could muster, "I'm not a girl. I'm a boy."

His outburst convulsed both men. When he stopped laughing, the big man finished the contents of the jar and spit a few bones into the water. "Another hour or so it'll be dark. Might as well stay right where we are for the night."

In another five minutes the yawl was at the side of the *Delta Belle*. Two ropes, hanging from the winch above, were fixed to hooks on the yawl, and the creaking winch began hauling them up.

Albie tried once more to find the house among the trees. He knew it was there, somewhere in that maze, but he couldn't locate it.

Did Alice know yet that he'd deserted her?

CHAPTER 8

"Ugh! . . . Ugh! . . . Ugh!"

With each grunt from the deck above, the yawl with
Albie and the two men in it was drawn out of the
brown water and, inch by jerking inch, up the not
white but gray algae and barnacle-encrusted hull of the
Delta Belle. Each "Ugh!" was followed by a squeal
from the winch.

When the yawl reached the level of the deck and the
big man stepped over the rusted rail, Albie followed

him. He and Frederick were left to unload. He followed Frederick's grumbling instructions about where he should deposit the food, and during his movement along a passageway, from one cabin to another, he saw that the repairs Frederick had referred to had never been completed, if, indeed, they'd ever been begun.

Long sections of the railing were missing. The stairs leading to the boiler deck were unusable, and a rope ladder hung from the rail above, to be used in their place. The housing that once had covered the starboard paddle wheel was nonexistent, except for three boards, the condition of which suggested that someone had decided the job was not worth completing.

Several of the wheel's buckets visible above the water were either cracked or totally missing. Even in the blue-gold twilight Albie could see that this was not one of those "floating palaces" described that night by that salesman from Duluth. *That* night. How long ago, how far away, *that* night seemed now!

That night, accepting the offer of bed and board until the end of the blizzard, the salesman had repaid his obligations by entertaining Albie and his parents with descriptions of the life offered to passengers who could afford to travel first class by boat rather than by stagecoach.

Permitted to stay up long past his bedtime for the unique opportunity to acquire education and culture simultaneously, Albie sat in front of the fire, with the wind outside howling in protest at being excluded.

"One of the finest," that salesman had said, "is the *General Pike*. The saloon is supported by eight marble columns. Carpets as fine as any in London's palaces. Crimson berth curtains, mirrors beyond count, paintings and furniture elegant beyond belief. And the most ornate chandeliers a man's mind can conceive."

Albie's mother had managed to lift herself out of her reverie to to ask if, in such display, the food weren't sure to be disappointing.

"Madame," the salesman had whispered. "On several boats on the Mississippi, I have seen, at a single meal, thirty-one different dishes placed before twenty-two passengers. Tables literally covered with dishes wedged closer together than the hairs on that hound at your young son's feet. I recall on the *Telegraph No. 1* a bill of fare offering three soups, five kinds of fish, six kinds of boiled meats (several with sauces), eleven entries consisting of meats and baked dishes and including such delicacies as . . . and forgive my pronunciation—I am not a native Frenchman . . . Calves Head à la Tortul, Giblets à la Glassey, Boneta la Paysanne, Veal à la Chasseur, Bone Ducks à la Chamford, Pula à la Anglais, Chickens à la Diable, Macaroni Parisienne, Galatin à la Saute, Venison à la Crapsden, Quails à la Du Price."

That evening Albie had gone to bed with a firm determination that at the first opportunity he was leaving that secluded farm for the excitement and romance of the world east of those desolate prairies and forests, and though that determination had faded, the dreams cultivated by that evening had remained as glorious as ever. How many evenings, after hours in a hot field, he had slept on fantasies of steamboats like the *General Pike* and the *Telegraph No. 1*, fantasies of his sitting at tables groaning under dishes with such foreign titles as recited that night in front of the fire by that mustachioed salesman from Duluth, the capitol, to Albie, of the entire civilized world.

Well, the *Delta Belle* was no *General Pike*, that was certain.

Prodded by the big man, after the yawl had been emptied, Albie followed on the heels of the smaller Frederick. An odor of dung and putrefied flesh hung so heavy in the air that his fingers could almost feel it. From the forward part of the boat a variety of animals . . . cattle, sheep, goats, pigs, horses, ducks, turkeys, chickens . . . were calling bleakly and half-heartedly to each other. As the wind shifted, mingling sounds with smells, Albie knew that the odor and the sounds were coming from the same source.

A twisted gnome of a figure swathed in a grotesque collection of cloth appeared on deck as if he'd been projected from the dark inner depths of the boat. His coarsely featured face, like his hands and his clothes, was covered with grease and grime. An aroma of oil surrounded his body like a thin suit of armor. By comparison, his two companions appeared clean and debonair and well-tailored.

"This all you found?" he called in a cracked, hoarse whisper. "That's all we need now. A kid. They're bad luck on a boat, kids are. Well, maybe he'll come in useful, maybe he will. Tee hee. First thing in the morning he'll help wood this piece of rust you call a boat. Tee hee."

The strange sounds that punctuated his speech were not so much giggles or spurts of laughter as they were sharp, clicking spits of breath formed by tapping the tip of his tongue against his teeth.

The big man seemed amused by him. He threw back his head and laughed. "Stop your complainin', Spider. This kid just might turn out the most profitable haul we made all week."

Spider thrust his face close to Albie's. "Tee hee. You don't have to say another word, Big Rafe. Not another word. I catch your plan right off." And Spider, whose webbed gray features must have given rise to his name, jabbed out a hand to grab at Albie's biceps. "His folks got money. His bones tell me. And his clothes. By gum, Big Rafe, you are a smart one. You are for sure. Tee hee." The foul breath, smelling of decayed flies, whistled through his fly-specked gums. "Whatsa matter? You scared of old Spider? Huh? Tee hee."

That was their plan. They meant to hold him for ransom. They'd had no intention whatever of rescuing him, of saving him. Why, they would have left him in the house without the slightest hesitation or concern. They would have taken the food and left him to starve to death. He glanced back at the island of trees and snags, thinking of how he'd been frightened of the lion and how he wished, now, he were back there with her. How clean the lion seemed by comparison.

"Get along," Big Rafe called, gripping Albie's arm so tightly that Albie winced.

First Spider and then Frederick picked their way

115

across the deck, along a narrow path between high stacks of barrels and carts and crates and boxes and casks. At times the walls rose above Albie's head, leaning precariously, threatening to tumble and spill their contents onto the four people moving among them. In the rooms which, in the boat's former days of glory, must have been passenger quarters, there were tables and chairs and bureaus in various shapes and sizes, of mahogany and rosewood and oak and ebony, covered with intricately carved detail. Mirrors, large and small, simple and ornate, leaned against baroque lamps with shades of stained glass or brass or tin. Chandeliers hung from hooks that had been hammered into the ceilings, clinking and chiming as the boat rocked and dipped at the end of its anchor line. Clocks and pots and pans and china and silver filled to overflowing boxes stacked on every available flat surface. Bales of cotton and sacks of cornmeal and flour filled one room from wall to wall and from the floor almost to the ceiling. In a room completely protected from the rain were bolts of yard goods, boxes of dresses and suits and shoes and hats and boots, and at least twenty new, still unstained saddles.

Spider and Frederick made their way without too much effort, and Albie followed them easily, but Big Rafe had to grunt and thrust with his shoulders and then pump with his heavy legs to make any progress through the narrow aisle.

They finally reached the rope ladder. Spider climbed with the agility of his namesake, and even Frederick moved with surprising speed. Albie climbed next, making his way up the rungs with aching hands and arms.

He'd not realized how weak he'd grown. In the last few days he'd eaten irregularly and infrequently. His sleep had never really been restful. Now the lack of food and rest was beginning to take its toll. He would have fallen or at least climbed back down had Big Rafe not let out a warning bellow louder than any being produced by the animals in the bow. With a final spurt, Albie made the last four or five feet and hauled himself onto the deck, which, at this level, was clear.

In the dim blue-gray light Albie could make out the animals crowded together at the bow, on the deck below, packed shoulder to shoulder from rail to rail, the chickens and other fowl cooped in crates and boxes and baskets. From the single quick view it seemed the animals were tied to each other as well as to capstans and rails. There had to be at least a hundred tied by their necks and heads and legs. From the volume of their noise, goats almost certainly outnumbered horses, cows, and pigs. Albie could only guess how long they'd been on board, but he did not have to guess to know that they'd not received much, if any, attention. Their portion of the boat had certainly not been cleaned. Now that the rain had stopped and the soaked dung had been exposed to the sun, the stench was enough to overwhelm even the strongest-willed farmer. There had to be a dead animal, or animals, among them, the decay of their bodies adding to the general odor.

The three men, unaffected, forced Albie into a room which, at one time, must have been a handsome pilot's

117

cabin. Now the glass was so heavily plastered with grime that a pilot could only maneuver the ship by guess.

The remains of perhaps a hundred meals covered a long table in the center of the room. Cups and plates were scattered among pots and jars and forks and spoons. Not an inch of the table surface was visible. There seemed to be no space for even one more spoon. But space was provided instantly by a swing of Big Rafe's arm. Glasses and cups shattered as they struck the floor. The food and fluid added one more layer to the several layers that had already created the thick, gummy carpet covering the floor.

Frederick and Big Rafe dropped into chairs at the side of the table. In response to a request from Big Rafe, Spider obligingly carried a large pewter pitcher to a whisky barrel. He returned with the pitcher and set it on the table, in the space cleared by Big Rafe, and then he, too, dragged up a chair. They selected mugs or glasses from among those already on the table, threw the previous contents in the general direction of a large iron bucket, and proceded to consume the whisky as if it were water.

Uncertain of what was expected of him, Albie stood at first near the entry and then, when it became obvious that no one was about to offer him either food or drink, or even suggest he sit somewhere, he decided to remove a box of marbelized glass doorknobs from a chair. He collapsed onto the seat and closed his eyes, fighting to break free of the lethargy and near nausea in which he was floundering.

Each of the three men took their turns at a loaf of bread and stuffing the pieces they'd torn, with meat sliced from what must originally have been a ten- or fifteen-pound ham, into their mouths. There was more growling and crunching and gurgling at the table than there was when Alice ate her food.

Alice.

He'd almost succeeded in forgetting her. Now he not only thought of her, he also wondered how he might return to her. He had to get back, he had to get food to her. Certainly he must have become identified in her mind as her provider. Was she waiting for him to appear with food now? Was she pacing the hall, sniffing the cupboards, growling out her impatience?

"Here," Big Rafe said, extending a knife on the end of which a thick wedge of ham was pinned. "You gotta be alive to be any use. Eat it."

Albie accepted the meat, but even at arm's length it almost succeeded in accomplishing what, so far, the odor from the bow of the ship had not accomplished. The men paid no attention to him as they filled and refilled their glasses.

One more slice of meat would not be noticed among the debris on the table. He lowered the ham into a mug of what could have been beer or coffee or vegetable soup, and then he resigned himself to watching the men get drunk.

Spider was reminiscing about his past, his trembling voice broken apart every few minutes to offer space for those occasional tee hees. His account of his insights and indignities made no impression on Big Rafe or Fred-

119

erick, each of whom alternated long periods of silence with charges of the other's incompetence or praise of their own unappreciated talents.

While the candles flickered and the shadows leaped and danced across the walls and threw bizarre shapes on the ceiling, Albie closed his eyes and desperately tried not to think of Alice prowling the floors of the old house so close and yet so far away.

". . . started with an Evans engine," Spider was muttering. "An Evans engine and one month's experience and I was workin' like a ten-year veteran . . ."

"Frederick, I remember," Big Rafe said, as if Spider's continuing monologue was totally silent, "I remember you was slidin' your skinny shins along the bar and I came in, I remember, and I said, 'I got an idea.'"

And Spider continued. "The engineer, he takes the orders from the captain and the pilot, and there's an accident, who gets it in the neck? Huh? Who? The engineer, in that boiler room, that's who. But I'm, tee hee, I'm tellin you . . ."

Frederick stirred out of his boozy silence just enough to open one eye. "Now, Big Rafe, you comes in that saloon and you says, 'Whatta you think, Frederick, about you and me works some profit outa this flood?' and I, it's *me*, Rafe, I says, 'Big Rafe, I got an idea. I knows where there's this old side-wheeler, called the *Delta Belle*. She's just rottin' away, but she's got maybe six months' work in her broken old bones' . . ."

And Spider, confiding his story to his half-empty whisky glass, ignoring the other two men as they ignored him, continued. "The engines and the boilers workin' away to get that boat up the rivers, against the current, through storms, up rapids, over bars, crashin' into snags and banks and other boats, with leakin' joints, cracked steam pipes, blown-out cylinder heads, broken shafts or wheel arms or jammin' rods, why, I've seen men they was engineers, tee hee, they grow gray-haired overnight. But not me, not old Spider. Look at this head of hair."

"And anyway, Big Rafe, I might be little, but that's why I learns to use my brain, and it's *my* brain thinks of old Spider here, the best engineer . . ."

"Tee hee, the Captain signaled start and then stop and then change speed and then reverse engines, them bells tellin' me, 'Stop, back, come ahead again, slow, come ahead full steam, stop, back off again, come ahead.' Always makin' sure I got steam left in my boilers . . ."

"*You* thought of Spider? *You?* Why, I've known that stunted old polecat since before he got his back busted in that boiler explosion. I've traveled up and down the Mississippi and the Ohio more times with him than you got hairs in your eyebrows. It was *me* said, 'Let's get Spider.' *I* knew he could run the *Delta Belle* over cows and the old boat'd think it was water smooth as a baby's bottom."

"I'll tell you," Spider confided to his now empty glass, "you gotta be careful, in floods, cause the water's loaded with sand and silt and it gets in the boilers, and you gotta clean them once, twice a day or they explode. I know twenty engineers, at least twenty, killed cause they put off cleanin' their boilers. Then someone invents this blowout valve and mud drum and, well, it ain't what it was when I was a striker, learnin' how, tee hee, to keep even rocks a-floatin'."

"You mighta knowed old Spider longer, Big Rafe, but who was it says there's gold floatin' into the Gulf in all them houses? Huh? Now, be honest, Big Rafe."

"Wood cost so much to burn and you couldn't get nothin' but cottonwood sometimes. Some engineers, they'll tell you oak or beech or ash or chestnut's the best, but it comes to wood, just plain wood, give old Spider pine. With plenty pitch. I recalls payin' seven dollars a cord above Sioux City and, tee hee, usin' thirty cords a day. I was the first engineer on the river, tee hee, to mix coal and wood. Now that'll put out heat for you . . ."

"You didn't even want us to hold this kid at first."

". . . and snags, tree trunks fifty, a hundred feet long, weighing maybe forty, fifty tons. A snag rips through the hull, that boat's gonna sink. I was on deck the day the *Samuel Claremont* hit a snag. Whole hull ripped open. Most passengers was asleep. Alarm sounded and the boat started sinkin' . . ."

"*I* didn't want to hold the kid? Blast you, Big Rafe, *I* was the one first brung it up . . ."

"Some passengers, they got to the hurricane deck. In two minutes the bow was sunk in the water below the guards. Passengers on lower decks drowned in their beds. Boat just threw off the boilers. Hull separated from the cabin and upper works and stacks fell away.

122

So'd the hurricane deck. Men, women, children thrown in the water and drowned. Yes, sir, I seen plenty, I have, tee hee. And I ain't through."

"Big Rafe, you wasn't so big I'd put my foot . . ."

Their speech was stumbling, slurring, slowing, but they continued filling their glasses. Spider fell first, his head dropping onto the table with a loud thump, knocking over his glass. Its contents carried soggy crumbs and half-chewed pieces of meat and slices of onion and yellowed egg shells into his hair and beard and inside the collar of his jacket and down his back. He started snoring.

Frederick, though he continued to open his mouth and work his lips, like a fish nibbling at the air that's drowning it, produced no sound. He leaned back too far, the chair tilted over, and he remained the way he landed: feet straight up in the air, the weight of his body on his shoulders and neck, head twisted, eyes open and staring at the shadow dance of the candle flames on the ceiling.

Ten minutes later Big Rafe dropped his glass. It struck the table, bounced, landed on the floor, bounced twice and then shattered. His body slid, inch by inch, down, down, down in his chair, his arms stiff at his sides. The distorted face dropped as far as the heavy black cushion of beard would permit it. His eyes, wide open, rolled around and around and then from side to side, as one bubbly belch alternated with every ten or fifteen wall-shaking snores.

Albie left his chair. Picking his way carefully, so he'd

not cut his feet, he eased past and over the collection of tangled legs and arms until he was out on deck.

The air was cool and sweet. A crisp, favorable wind protected him from the poisonous odors in the bow. The bright half moon hung from the fluffy end of a cloud, converting the brown ocean into a swell of luminous silver. From the rail, he saw the island of trees more distinctly now than he had a few hours before.

As he stood there, Albie noticed a foamy wake sparkling on the silver surface of the water. The wake trailed away, in the shape of a V, from its point, which was traveling toward the *Delta Belle*. He watched, spellbound, until the point of the V arrived at the boat. Alice!

The lion peered up at him and scratched at the hull in an effort to find a foothold. She kept slipping away each time, to swim toward the bow, toward the stern, and then to the side, to try to climb the moist, algae-covered hulk of the boat.

Albie dashed to the bow. The animals, subdued by exhaustion, exposure, starvation, thirst, barely protested his presence. Two or three chickens, flying at the walls of their boxes and baskets, attempted a moderately desperate cackle.

In a few seconds Albie had a sow untied. He pulled and pushed the grunting animal, kicked it and pleaded with it, lifted and tumbled it, until, finally, he had it at the rail. The apathetic pig had not squealed once, but as it sailed through the air, it seemed to sense its ordeal was over. Its squeal suggested relief, almost joy, rather than fright. The squeal ended the moment the pig struck the water.

A new foaming wake on the surface of the water was shaped again like a V. But this time the point of the V reversed, moving toward the island of snags that sheltered the house and Alice's babies.

CHAPTER 9

Albie awakened to the sound of coughing and cursing.

"The kid's gone. Spider . . . Frederick . . . wake up, you scum. You drunk yourselves under and you let the kid escape."

The voices of the other two men, first pained and then resentful, begged Big Rafe to let them sleep. They were sick. Let the kid go. It didn't matter. They had more than enough to get them all a stake out west.

But Big Rafe, unaware that Albie was less than twenty feet away, bellowed that they'd better damn well get up or he'd drag them by their damn miserable dirty necks. Frederick, trying to appease Big Rafe, pointed out the yawl. "He couldn'ta gone back to the house. Even a man, a good swimmer, couldn't buck that current."

"He must be on the boat," Spider said. The words were delivered as if his jaws ached.

"I didn't say he wasn't." That was Big Rafe. "But you better damn well find him, or I'll cut your throats from your ears to your boots."

The door burst open on the room where Albie had slept the night before. The sacks of meal and flour had offered the most comfortable surface he could find, but the scurry of rats, their persistent and constant gnawing, their squeaking feuds, had kept him awake until dawn.

"Here he is. Tee hee. You can't hide from old Spider, I'll tell you. Here he is, Big Rafe."

Albie let himself be tugged and pushed into the sunlight, accepting their curses and their threats. Big Rafe ordered Spider to get the boat moving, and Spider reminded him that before the day was over, they'd have to find a shoreline and haul at least ten cords of firewood on board. Then he ran at the rope ladder, grabbed a rung, and hauled himself up so fast that his hands and feet were a blur of motion.

Sitting on a pile of crates, Albie watched Frederick at the bow, making feeble efforts to feed the animals, or at least some of them. Albie wondered how long it would take Spider to discover what he'd done during the night.

128

Big Rafe appeared with several leather bags, *U.S. Mail Service* stamped on their sides. He upended one bag and emptied it onto the deck. There were several small packages, hundreds of letters, and about ten bundles of envelopes wrapped in wax paper and closed with legal-looking seals. Big Rafe opened the packages and letters first, extracting money and tossing all else into the air. Pieces of paper and envelopes sailed across the deck, over the rail, and into the water below. Most but not all of the money was returned to the leather bag. Some went into Big Rafe's shirt pocket. He glanced at Albie and said nothing, but Albie knew it would be at the risk of his life to even pretend he knew what was happening. From the wax-paper-covered envelopes he took heavy pieces of parchment, all of which he examined and then deposited in the mail bag.

After Big Rafe worked for almost an hour Frederick joined him, to work alongside him. Since he could not read, he could only extract the money, all of which, under the eye of Big Rafe, he conscientiously returned to the leather bag. He gave over all the parchment papers to Big Rafe, who examined them, nodded approvingly, and shrugged them over the rail or indicated they be kept.

"I wish I knew about stocks and bonds," Frederick said. "How'd you ever learn them, Big Rafe?"

Big Rafe growled, probably angry over Frederick's presence, which prohibited his diverting some of the money into his pocket. "First off," he said, "you gotta be able to read."

Frederick, rubbing his hands, laughed, as if it were a

joke he had the talent to appreciate. He asked Big Rafe how much they'd get when they cashed in their bonds, but Big Rafe insisted the whole procedure was too complex to explain to someone who couldn't read or who had no experience in the operations of big business.

"Just a guess," Frederick persisted. "Come on. Just a guess. How much we got so far in them stocks and bonds?"

"Rough guess, oh, maybe five thousand dollars."

Frederick slammed his hands together and howled with glee. "Five thousand dollars. And cash? How much in cash, Big Rafe? Just a rough guess."

"Well, maybe . . . oh, about five hundred dollars in that bag. And maybe a thousand in the other bags we went through yesterday."

Frederick whistled. He shook his head, startled, and he repeated the word *thousand* reverently. He held out a paper he'd removed from an envelope and asked, "What's this, Big Rafe?"

Big Rafe accepted it and studied it and returned it. "A picture. What's it look like?"

"I know it's a picture. I ain't dumb, Big Rafe. But what's it a picture *of?*"

"It's from a magazine," Big Rafe growled. "Called *Harper's Weekly*. It shows Abe Lincoln debatin' the Little Giant."

"The Little Giant?"

"You don't know who that is? Don't you know what's goin' on in this country? No wonder the country's in bad shape. People like you, don't know about stocks and bonds, can't read, don't know what's goin' on in your own country, that's why the country's in such bad shape."

"I don't think the country's in bad shape. Look at us. We ain't in bad shape, we're in good shape. And anyway, what's the Little Giant? Who is he? What are they debatin'?"

Big Rafe waved away the possibility of discussion as if it would be of no use and Frederick started to protest, but his protest was cut short by the sudden snort of the boilers and the spill of black smoke from the stack. The boat took on a reverberation that matched the working boilers. It tugged gently at its anchor line, anxious to get back into a contest with the river. Then the boat bucked twice like an angry horse. The stack gave one final belch of black smoke and sent out a rolling spray of gray powder. The boat stopped moving.

Big Rafe looked up toward the boiler deck. He complained that Frederick's babbling was distracting him. He suggested that Frederick go up to the boiler deck to help Spider, but at that moment Spider appeared at the rail.

Big Rafe waved a fist at him. "Let's get this boat movin'. We shoulda been ten miles from here by now. I bet you been asleep up there. Another day or two the water's gonna be down and we'll be here on dry land."

"Big Rafe, we got trouble."

Big Rafe waited, his fist, clamped over several pieces of currency, pounding at his thigh.

"Can't figure it out," Spider said. "Spur and bevel

gears, you know, they connect the main shaft and rotary . . ."

"Don't give me all them words. They don't mean nothin' to me."

"Gear teeth broke," Spider said.

"Fix them. You got tools up there."

"Big Rafe, things like this take time. And I ain't got tools that . . ."

"Get it fixed and let's get movin'. We lost a whole day already. Frederick, go give that so-called engineer a hand."

Frederick dashed off. As soon as he was up the ladder and out of sight, Big Rafe stuffed the fistful of money into a pocket of his trousers, not bothering this time to give Albie a warning glance.

Albie lounged on the crates, dozing in the warm sunlight. At least Alice was not starving. She'd broken that pig's neck last night and had towed it back to the house and, with her belly full, was probably dozing right now, as he was. But she was probably feeling strong, comfortably maternal, secure. Unlike him she probably was not thinking beyond the present moment. Or was she? Did she plan what she would do when the time came to move her babies? Was she preparing them to surrender to their confinement in that house, to their exile from those trees and fields in which she'd once roamed, in which their father was roaming now?

He could see the gray wisps of smoke oozing out of the stack. Did Spider have any idea how those gears had so suddenly shattered? Had he found that piece of chisel that had been wedged between the teeth of the two large gears? And if he had, would he say anything about it? Albie doubted he would. He was relying on Spider's fear that he himself might be blamed for having absently dropped the tool during his daily routines. In any case, the boat would not be moving. Unless Spider was a genius, it might never move again. In the meantime, Albie would have more time to think and plan. If the rain did not begin again, if the river kept going down, if boats started moving along the river . . .

"Could I have some water?" he asked. He had no desire for food, but he was thirsty.

Without lifting his eyes Big Rafe said, "Whole river out there. Go get yourself some."

Albie lay back and closed his eyes, wondering if, were he given the chance, he'd grab the rifle lying near Big Rafe's foot. If he had the rifle, he could force the men to take him ashore. He didn't know how far away the shore was, but they'd know. Once he was ashore, how would he get Alice there? And her cubs?

"Up in the pilot house," Big Rafe said. "There's water up there. And bring me back a pitcher of redeye."

Albie climbed the rope ladder tied to the rail posts of the boiler deck. He held his breath as long as he could when he entered the pilot house, and he tried to keep from looking at the table. There were so many barrels and pots and crocks on every surface that he did not know where to start looking. Everything he touched was either oily or sticky, surrounded with moldy remnants of food, or filled with substances that could not possibly be fluid.

He found a large crock that was partially covered

with a lid. An enameled dipper lay across the lid. Because there were fewer flies interested in the contents, he decided that the crock was more likely to be filled with water. He lifted the lid and peeked in. The sorry gray liquid had to be water; it was the least repulsive substance available. Try as he might, as thirsty as he was, he could drink no more than half a dipper of the water.

He tugged a cut-glass pitcher loose from its base of grease and gum and held it under the spigot on the whisky barrel.

He managed to descend the rope ladder without spilling much of the whisky, and he handed the pitcher to Big Rafe, who, sitting on the crates where Albie had been lounging, was paring his fingernails with a large penknife.

Big Rafe drank straight from the pitcher, swallowed four times, removed the pitcher from his mouth, belched, and swallowed again. When he stopped to rest the pitcher in his lap, he glowered down at Albie. "How do we get word to your folks?"

"I don't know."

"We could send a letter. But I don't trust the *U.S. Mail Service.*" He said it as if the phrase were in capital letters. "We could send word with a messenger. Someone going that way. It'll take time. And we gotta hold on to you all the while. Could be four or five months."

"You think my mom and dad have money. They don't."

"No?"

134

"They don't. Honest."

"They own a farm?"

"Yes."

"Is it built up?"

"Everything was flooded out. All the buildings, all the animals, everything."

Big Rafe stared at him. As he drank, again and again, he seemed to be considering what Albie had just said.

"Big Rafe."

He turned his head, the pitcher attached to his mouth. His eyes were now so bloodshot that the pupils were almost lost in the red orbs.

Spider and Frederick were standing there, side by side. Spider was wiping his hands on a piece of cloth. Both hands and the cloth were so greasy that it was impossible to know where flesh ended and cloth began.

"Bad news, Big Rafe," Frederick said.

Big Rafe waited.

Spider shook his head, his webbed features heavy with gloom. "The camshaft, too."

"What about the camshaft?"

"Where it's attached to the rock-shaft?"

"What about where it's attached to the rock-shaft?"

"It's not attached any more. We can't reverse. Unless . . ."

Big Rafe slammed his pitcher on the crate and fixed Spider with an accusing sneer, as if he knew Spider, for some perverse reason, had broken the camshaft himself.

"Can you fix it?"

"It'll take all day. And then it might not . . ."

"Well, what are you waitin' for? Get to work."

Spider started off but then returned to lift the pitcher and drink greedily. The liquid ran down his cheeks, down his neck, and across his chest.

Frederick took the pitcher next and drank his share. "I maybe oughta help him," Frederick said. "Some of them pieces, especially them hooks, they're too heavy for a runt like him."

Big Rafe, his eyes beginning to narrow and his voice growing rough and raw-edged, handed Albie his pitcher.

When Albie returned, Frederick was standing beside Big Rafe. They'd been discussing him, he knew. He offered Big Rafe the pitcher, but Frederick pulled it from his hand, cursing. He pointed a long, skinny, grease-covered finger at Albie. "We ought to just throw you overboard."

"I ain't in favor," Spider said. "Killin' oughta be accidental."

"Might just do that," Big Rafe said. "Seems to me we got nothin' but bad luck since he came on board."

"That's what does it."

"Like a woman. Women and kids, they're bad luck on boats."

"That's right, Big Rafe. That camshaft was fine last night. Today, after that kid comes on board, it's broke. Can't tell me there's no connection."

"Spider said we'll be needing wood. Maybe we oughta feed him into the furnace. He's about as big as one of them logs we burn."

Albie backed up, his face white, and then he whirled and ran, climbing the ladder so swiftly that Big Rafe and Frederick burst into laughter. "Look at him go . . . he's not a boy, he's a monkey . . . ha ha ha, he don't like fires, Big Rafe . . . ha, ha . . ."

Albie threw himself over the rail of the boiler deck and raced along the passageway to the barely attached stairs leading above to the hurricane deck. He raced past the pilot house, unwilling, unable, to enter that garbage-filled room, and he threw himself into the texas, a small portion of cabin space behind the pilot house. Not having been used for storage or sleeping or eating, the texas was empty except for a broken chair and scraps of old newspapers and magazines.

Albie slammed the door and leaned against it, breathing heavily. Then he slid to the floor. He sat there, staring into space. What could he do?

The men had no intention of putting him on land, not even if they decided against holding him for ransom. To let him free would be too great a risk. They could not chance his telling what he knew. But what, indeed, did he know?

He knew they were robbers. Thieves. And probably killers. Why not? They'd been scavenging during the flood, living off the misfortunes of others, pillaging houses floating down the river and, apparently, looting stranded boats as well. Where else would they have gotten their cargo? The mail bags? The animals?

If they were caught and convicted just for the theft of the U.S. mail, they'd be put in prison for years. Maybe they'd even be hung. What difference would it make if they now added murder to their crimes? And especially if it were a murder for which they would probably never be convicted. Meaning, and Albie shuddered as he considered the fact, meaning that they could murder him (and so protect themselves) and then simply throw his body over the side. No one would ever know. They, the three men, could never be blamed.

Through the thin walls of the texas Albie could hear the men laughing. They were drinking again, forgetting the work required on the camshaft. Sooner or later one of them, in a drunken stupor, would decide it was time to come looking for him. When they found him, they'd probably, in their drunken stupor, even torture him before putting him to death.

He couldn't just sit here, waiting for them. He had to hide. But where? He couldn't chance the boiler or hurricane decks. Spider and Frederick and Big Rafe would scour each room, every inch of which they were familiar with, until they discovered his hiding place. The main deck? One of those rooms offered the best chance. Behind or inside one of the boxes, or burrowed down under a crate or behind heavy sacks of flour or cornmeal. That was the best. They'd never suspect he'd be under their noses. But he'd have to get there without their seeing him. Then, at the first chance, he'd dive overboard and try to swim to the island. He'd probably not make it. He'd probably drown. But at least he'd be trying. He'd be fighting. He'd not just be passively waiting for them to come kill him.

Albie opened the door and crawled, on his hands and knees, toward the rail. He lay on his belly and moved forward until he could see the tops of the three heads. Yes, Spider was there. They were sitting where he'd left them, entertaining each other with descriptions of how the kid had skittered up that ladder like a monkey.

Edging back and then rising, Albie went to the port side of the boat. It was a drop of about twelve feet to the deck. He couldn't chance it. Not yet, anyway. They'd hear him landing. He might even break his leg. Then he would be through. He searched the area, as far as he could chance it, for rope or wire, but he found nothing.

On his hands and knees, on his belly, darting from wall to wall, door to door, he reached the most forward part of the deck overlooking the main deck where, below, the animals were herded together. The sunlight was warm now, almost hot, and the stench, striking him in the face like the blast from an oven, brought a groan from his throat. He closed his eyes and slid backward, turning his face away, waiting for his stomach to settle again. How many dead animals were there among the live ones?

The moment the idea came to him, the moment the audacity of it struck him and the knowledge that he was sure to be safe if he did it, Albie rose to his knees, raced forward, and leaped, trying to guide the fall of his body so he'd land between two animals rather than on one of them. His hip struck the rump of a cow, glanced off, and he landed on his feet in the thick pad of dung and rotted hay. For one moment there was an outburst of noise, but the animals were so exhausted by the exertion, so near collapse from hunger, that they soon returned to their silent contemplation of advancing death.

Albie crawled on his hands and knees, between the legs and under the bellies of horses and cows. His hands and legs sank to his elbows and thighs in the mud, but he continued moving. By now the odor was not so much odor as taste and not so much taste as essence, a simple, palpable essence that existed around him as water would have existed were he floating or swimming in the river. He refused to think, forbade himself to feel. If he took time to think or feel now, he'd be sick. If he let himself be sick here, in the midst of these dying animals, he, too, would die. And he was determined to live, to live and to escape and to return to the house and to help keep Alice and her cubs live and, eventually, even if took months or years, to find his way home.

In the midst of this heavy presence of death, Albie chose to fight to live.

A mound of what he thought to be dung or straw proved to be the decaying body of a calf. He recoiled after his hands sank into the distended belly and, without agony or disgust, he simply rerouted his advance so that he edged around the maggot-filled carcass. When he reached the edge of the deck, which decided the limits of the herd, Albie lay flat.

Frederick, aroused by the brief outburst from the animals, had left the crates where he and Big Rafe and Spider were drinking. He stood near the animals, calling them names and kicking them. "You stinking bunch of hyenas, shut up. Another day, one more day, and you'll be running around on land and we'll be richer for it. Here. Stop your bellerin'." From a stack of bales in a nearby cabin, he threw several forks of hay into the middle of the herd and tossed a few handfuls of corn into the crates and baskets containing the fowl. He walked among them with water collected by dropping a bucket on a rope into the river. He filled an occasional iron pot. Albie thought Frederick might see him when some of the animals trampled on others in their rush for food and water, but at the last moment, his shin grazed by a hoof, Frederick struck a horse with the bucket and turned away. "To hell with you. Go ahead and die. I got enough. Who needs the few dollars you skinny weasels'll get me?" And he limped away, rubbing his shinbone and cursing.

Albie recovered the bucket and for the rest of the afternoon occupied his time hauling water for all the animals. The water not only served to quench the animals' thirst, it also served to keep them quiet. There was no need for Frederick to come and abuse them again.

All afternoon, as he worked, Albie heard the men searching the ship, exchanging curses and blame for his escape. Finally Big Rafe announced, "He ain't on the ship. He can't be."

They stood on the main deck, at the rail, weaving and growling and cursing in their drunkenness and assuring each other that the kid was where he deserved to be for bringing them bad luck. Frederick said he was just one more bloated body floating in the Mississippi, and Spider was concerned about maybe the kid's death couldn't be considered accidental and they might just get paid back somehow. Big Rafe bellowed that he wasn't interested in having any preachers on his boat, and Spider assured him he wasn't any preacher, but there was such a thing as God and you didn't have to be a preacher to believe . . .

"Get up there," Big Rafe ordered. "Get this boat movin'."

Spider, giggling as if he enjoyed his role as target for Big Rafe's anger, trotted back to the boilers. Albie waited, knowing what he had to do.

CHAPTER 10

The sun, hot red, slid toward the horizon, spilling fire over sky, water, boat. The island, refusing to ignite, pushed its grotesque black profile up through the glow. The walls of the *Delta Belle* that had once been white were now pink, reflecting the setting sun.

Spider had been hammering and grinding metal in the boiler room for the last hour. Abruptly, he stopped.

Peering over the spine of a groaning, heavy-headed cow, Albie saw Spider come out of the boiler room.

143

"Hey, Rafe," Spider called. "Hey, Big Rafe." When his call received no reply, Spider's voice grew angrier, more insistent. "Big Rafe, hey, where are you? I got good news. . ."

What, Albie wondered, could that good news be? Had his plan failed? Had the chisel he'd placed in the gears not done its job? Had Spider, in his workshop, repaired the damage, and was the *Delta Belle* about to sail?

Albie chanced attracting Spider's attention by picking his way through the muck, placing his hands and feet carefully so he'd not disturb the weary, barely living animals. In their misery the animals made way for him, as if they sensed his sympathies. Behind a long-bristled boar that had just collapsed onto its side, Albie raised up on his elbows to peer over the barely moving ribs. He had a clear view of the upper decks. There was Spider, just sober enough to place one foot in front of the other without falling. He entered the pilot house.

An hour later the vermilion sun balanced on the rim of the horizon, promising at any moment to slide behind the far edge forever. Spider was still inside the pilot house. From where Albie sat, the entire hulk of the *Delta Belle*, and every animal he could see, appeared to have been dipped in blood.

Now, Albie decided, now or never.

Moving silently, slowly, he tiptoed along the deck to the rope ladder. He waited at the bottom of the ladder, breathing hard—ready to run if he had to, ready to leap over the railing and into the red muddy water if he had to.

144

With one cautious hand after the other he picked his way up the ladder, wincing as the straining ropes squeaked and rubbed against the boards. He eased his head and then his eyes above the rim of the second deck. Nothing to be seen, nothing to be heard. He climbed over the rail, waiting, prepared. No one shouted, no one came rushing from the pilot house.

He eased his way along the walls to the entry of the pilot house and waited. He heard snoring and a collection of miscellaneous mutters, murmurs, grunts, and whistles that could only be produced by someone in the clutch of a nightmare, or someone in a drunken stupor. When he managed to force himself forward, so he might see inside the pilot house, he relaxed. There they sat, all three of them, erect and open-eyed but totally unconscious.

Albie returned to the rope ladder, descended to the main deck, and after a ten-minute search discovered several lengths and coils of rope in the boiler room. For a moment he considered another effort to sabotage the gears, but he decided against it. He'd not risk another second. He had to put his plan into action.

Carrying a long piece of rope, Albie climbed the ladder. He untied the knots of the stringers that held it secure, and he let the entire ladder drop to the deck below. After a single loop around the rail the rope hung in two strands down the wall. Both ends reached to within a few feet of the main deck. Perfect. By holding one strand in his hands and wrapping the other around his body and between his legs, Albie lowered himself, feeding one strand up through his hands. When he reached the end, he dropped the remaining three feet or four feet and pulled down the rope. If they came after him now, they'd have no way to get to the main deck except by jumping. And if they jumped, in their condition, they just might, if Albie were lucky, break their heads as well as their legs.

The next ten or fifteen minutes were spent wrestling the bulky, grease-slicked rope ladder to the rail of the main deck. He tied its three stringers to the rail supports and heaved the ladder over the side. The bottom rungs floated in the water.

Albie filled the yawl with the food they'd taken from the house, with, just in case, additional cans of hardtack and biscuits. He scurried back and forth, from room to room, torn between taking time to search out exactly what he needed and just grabbing things at random and escaping fast. He carried sections of a bale of hay across the deck and into the yawl and then, finally, he hurried back to the animals. Thinking that they were most likely to be docile and obedient, Albie freed two goats and lifted them into the yawl. They made no sound and they offered no resistance. Tied on a short tether to an oarlock, they settled down immediately and closed their eyes. An extra moment was required to fit the oars securely on the floor of the yawl so they'd not fall out.

Now the final and most dangerous part.

Albie pushed against the movable metal arm from which the yawl was suspended until the yawl hung clear of the rail. He took in a deep breath and began turning the wheel. One full turn, another, another. He watched the yawl, its hold ropes taut, settle lower and lower toward the water. Sweat dripped into his eyes, and his shoulder muscles twitched as he struggled to control and subdue the noise of the wheel.

In the forward part of the boat a cow called into the darkness, and a horse, probably gored by a horn, screamed and snorted. Other animals picked up the protests and added their own. Albie, looking up to see if anyone had been aroused in the pilot house, lost control of the wheel. It spun free, dropping the yawl with one long, shrill shriek and a final explosive splash.

Albie climbed over the rail. He caught his toes and then his fingers in the rope ladder and scurried down the side of the *Delta Belle* into the yawl. He managed, despite numb and quivering fingers, to free the ropes and hooks that fixed the yawl to the boat. He grabbed the oars, set them in the locks, and started rowing.

He caught himself in time, easing his stroke and trying to control his breathing. He'd have to try to outwit the still strong current by angling the yawl's course so he'd actually end up above the island, permitting the flow of the river to carry him into the network of trees. Glancing occasionally over his shoulder, Albie continued working to correct his course. If he should miss the island and be swept into the main body of the river, that, he knew, would be the end. He'd never be able to row upstream, to recover the distance lost. Fortunately, with the river having gone down the last few days, the current had also been weakened.

One more minute, perhaps two. That was as long as

he could continue. When his arms threatened to rebel, Albie tried to distract himself from thoughts of exhaustion by thinking of other days, other events. But even the effort to select silent words seemed to sap his strength. He tried to imagine what the river would be like after the water receded to its normal width and depth. Boats would use the river again. The snags would be removed first. Following that thought, as it had followed the thought before, came the recognition of Alice's doom. Whoever found him would also find Alice. And whoever would find her would surely shoot her. "Like Indians," his father had said once to Sam Abernathy, "the only good cougar is a dead cougar."

The image of Alice, sprawled as he'd seen other dead cougars sprawled, fled and returned and stayed. He bent over and closed his eyes, but there she was, lying on the floor of his parents' bedroom, eyes open and glazed, tongue fallen out of her mouth, a hole in her skull between those beautiful amber eyes. And there were the two cubs squirming inside the burlap bag; the bag, weighted with rocks, sinking down through the muddy water; the cubs choking and scratching at the burlap, trying to mew for relief and, in mewing, choking and bloating and bursting as the bag continued sinking.

Albie raised his head and looked back. He rowed furiously to make up for the drift that had occurred while he'd been torturing himself with those pictures of Alice and the cubs.

The space separating the *Delta Belle* from the island was no more than seventy or eighty yards, but in moving at a steep diagonal, Albie must have rowed twice that distance. He grunted and prayed for strength for one more stroke, then one more, then one . . . then, there was the water lapping at the trees. Branches tore his shirt and skin, but he barely felt the pain as he slumped over the oars. He could have dropped and stretched out and slept, but he still had work to do. He had to get the food and the goats to the house. When he tried to stand, he almost tumbled backward into the water. His legs and arms were numb. He looked down to see if his fingers were moving, but it was too dark to see them, to know if they were responding at all.

He sat for a while, to permit the strength and sense of touch to return. He looked about him as he waited and comforted himself with the thought that the night would be fairly warm. If the flood had struck a month earlier, he'd be frozen by now.

Which should he try to take first, one of the goats or one of the crates? As he tried to make that decision, he recognized another problem. More trees had been snared in the island trap since he'd left the house for the *Delta Belle.* They were now added to the bulk that had been collected before he'd left. In the darkness, even with the full moon, it would be almost impossible to find the house. Impossible and dangerous. One faulty step could drop him into the water, which was still flowing with enough strength to pull him through the tangled roots and branches into the sweep of the river. Having gone this far, there was no sense in risking his and Alice's survival by insisting he search the island tonight. With a sigh Albie settled next to the two goats. Still lying down, their eyes still closed, they gave no sign of protest when he snuggled close for warmth.

Several times throughout the night he awakened, chilled, and tried to burrow his way beneath the goats, to use them as a blanket, but they stumbled up, snorting in the moonlight, not strong enough to tug at their ropes or even to bleat. Eventually they returned, to seek him out and settle beside him.

He sat up once, thinking he heard voices from the *Delta Belle*. She rode the silver of the water like a ghost, blue-white, silent, so thin and light that she seemed almost ready to lift and float through the air. Surely, he thought, they knew by now he'd escaped. What would they do? Not much, since he had the yawl. They would probably sail off in the morning, glad to be rid of him. He lay back, staring into the moon, listening to the labored breathing of the goats.

The hot sun burning through his eyelids awakened Albie. He rubbed the sunspots out of his eyes. There, on the smooth surface of the river, so close he thought he could swim to it with a strong push and a few strokes, lay the *Delta Belle*. And beyond the boat, as if they'd erupted out of the water during the night, were slopes of green hills. A mile, perhaps a half mile, away. On the crests of those hills the tufted silhouettes of trees. The previous day of sunlight and the evening's dry wind had dissolved the last walls of fog.

Albie stood up in the yawl. He glanced just once at the *Delta Belle*, and, satisfied that they'd decided to accept his escape, he turned to the trees. Where within that forest, and it *was* a forest now, was the house? Perhaps the weight of the additional trees had crushed it. Or perhaps the house, pushed and pulled by the stress and strain of the shifting current, had worked itself free and was now floating down the river.

Albie stooped, squatted, stood on the seat, lay down, but no matter from what perspective he searched, he could not discover a line or angle or surface that might suggest a house. One thing, however, was certain. The river *had* gone down. The mud line on the trees, marking the greatest height to which the water had climbed, was more than three feet above the water's present level.

All right, the river was down; it would go down even more; land was visible; boats would soon be working the river . . . what could he do to guarantee survival until he had his feet on that land that was now in sight?

Wait. That was all he could do—and hope. Or pray. Or both. The *Delta Belle* was still silent. Could Big Rafe and Frederick and Spider still be unconscious? Had they awakened, only to drink themselves into another stupor? Or were they planning another raid on the house, to recapture him, so he might not be used as a witness against them should they ever be captured? No, they couldn't come after him, he remembered, because he had the yawl. And not even Big Rafe was likely to try to swim the river. Not yet, at least. Well, Albie decided, he'd have to keep an eye on the boat as well as the water.

The goats, their eyes closed against the light, nodded in their sleep. Or was it sleep? Were they dying?

Albie tore hay from the partial bale he'd brought for the animals, and he fed it to them by hand. They munched it slowly, as if they'd lost the urge to eat, as if it were not only impossible but also unwise to replenish the energy that had already been wasted. They chewed slowly, reluctantly, their ribs punching through their fur. In between bites, chews, swallows, they rested, their eyes still closed, panting heavily.

Albie opened a jar of his mother's stewed tomatoes. The juice tasted as sweet as syrup. The red pulp seemed to inject new strength into his body the moment it dropped into his stomach. He broke a piece of hardtack from a slab and munched it, amazed at the delight he felt in the powerful motions of his jaws, the grinding of his teeth, the taste of starch.

The sun, almost directly overhead now, was so warm that he began to perspire. He removed his shirt and sat near the goats, naked from the waist up, waiting.

Bits and pieces of twigs and boxes and lumber floated into the island, and then, finding no hold and giving in to the tug of the current, they drifted off. A tree as large as the one that had smashed through the house several days before drifted into view far up the river. If it continued in its present direction, the tree would pass between the island and the *Delta Belle*. If one of those unpredictable undercurrents shifted the body as much as a few feet, the tree could strike the island. If it did, it would almost certainly crush the yawl, with Albie in it.

He might have left the yawl and worked his way into the island, away from the center of impact, but he did not have that much time. He continued watching as the great tree, like some half-submerged prehistoric monster, sailed toward him, rolling, dipping, clawing at the sky. Then the tree turned, caught in a crosscurrent, showing its base and heavy roots and next its tufted, green-tipped crest. When it straightened again, it was closer not to the island but to the *Delta Belle*, drifting toward the boat's anchor line. At that moment a cry rang out from the *Delta Belle*. Two men appeared at the rail. One, Albie saw, was Big Rafe. The other had to be Frederick. They were frantically hauling up the line by hand, trying to pull the anchor clear of the water before the tree could catch it and could pull the boat down the river. A roar from Big Rafe sent Frederick, protesting loudly about his always having to do the hard work, over the rail and onto one of the branches.

The line was snarled in the very branch Fredrick was clinging to and climbing down. As Big Rafe continued roaring, the *Delta Belle*, yielding to the surging power of the drifting tree, began to turn. With a cry of victory Frederick freed the line and let it fall back into the water. The anchor caught again and held, and the *Delta Belle* stopped moving. Frederick, realizing suddenly he was adrift on the tree, stared at Big Rafe. Shouting, he turned to climb to a part of the tree that would be less dangerous, that would bring him closer to the *Delta Belle*, but at that moment the tree rolled, pitching him out into space. He fell into a tangle of limbs that

153

seemed, as Albie watched, to close like fingers about him. The tree continued rolling, carrying Frederick, screaming, under the surface of the water. Then, as if satisfied, the tree seemed to shake and stretch and settle in that position.

Big Rafe, and now Spider, stood at the rail of the *Delta Belle*, their hands shading their eyes, as they watched the tree continue its journey down the Mississippi.

Albie lay down in the yawl, and though the sun was hot on his bare chest, he felt cool. He closed his eyes, but there, imprinted on his eyelids, was the figure of Frederick trapped in the branches, drawn down and under. Albie drew his shirt over his body and shivered beneath it, working to clear his eyes of that trapped, flailing figure.

The growl was not so much a growl as it was a purr. He sat up, searched the trees, and finally found her. She was stretched out on a limb. How long she'd been lying there, observing him, he didn't know, but as he climbed, she turned and moved away, toward the interior of the island. He would, he decided, take a crate of food for himself first and come back for the goats next. He followed Alice as she moved from trunk to trunk, branch to branch. She stopped occasionally to look back at him.

The branches whipped and cut his body and the crate grew heavier, but Albie continued, following the lion, stepping carefully so he'd not fall into the still swirling, still hissing, brown water below. Then, as if during the blink of an eye it had been constructed, there was the house in front of him, so small and insignificant within the thick maze of forest he thought at first that part of it had been torn away. But no, it was all there, just as he'd left it.

The water had receded so far that the house was suspended above the water, held in the air by that long branch that had punctured its body that stormy night a thousand years ago.

Albie followed Alice onto the tree and through the ruptured wall into their house.

CHAPTER 11

The lion went directly to her cubs, and Albie went to his bedroom. He felt as if he were returning from a long trip. He'd stayed once, for a weekend, at the Abernathys, and on Monday morning, as he'd ridden Summer across the hills toward home, he'd kept waiting for the first sound of a voice, wondering if it would be Elizabeth's or Alice Anne's. It had been his mother's. She'd been standing in the doorway, waiting for him. Now he half expected his mother or father to appear as he walked down the hall.

A sense of hope had been building in him since he'd left the *Delta Belle*. When he'd seen, for the first time, the slopes of those dark green hills rising out of the brown water, his hopes had merged to form one swell of assurance. He'd felt then that escape from that still brown, still swollen, still threatening river was certain. He'd be on land in one or two days, or three. On land and on his way home. The assurance, until this minute, had been so strong, so real, so immediate that the appearance of his mother and father, of Elizabeth or Alice Anne, would have seemed natural.

Home. How he dreamed, longed, prayed for home, for that quiet, loving, peaceful life that had been his childhood and would continue to be his youth and his manhood. When he'd seen those dark green hills, *home* and *loving, peaceful life* had merged into one word, one sensation.

But now, in the house, hearing the hollow echoes of his bare feet, seeing again the twisted and broken walls with their torn and faded pennants of wallpaper, picking his way through the chaos left behind by Big Rafe and Frederick, Albie watched and felt that assurance being wrenched and shaken and almost destroyed. The shell of what had once been a home, the relics of Big Rafe and the too recently drowned Frederick, the branches of newly snagged trees clicking like loose grillwork at the window (closing him in, closing others, rescuers, out), challenged his faith. Why should he continue to believe that rescue was inevitable? He had, after all, constructed

158

that sense of assurance not on fact but on fantasy. What, factually, had really happened to give him cause for hope?

He tried to tell himself that escape from the *Delta Belle* and the decline of the flood waters were *facts* and *facts* were legitimate causes for hope. But the escape had simply exchanged hazards. A shift of the trees, a new storm, could complete the destruction of this house in the time it took to inhale a deep breath. And even if the house should survive, it was no guarantee that *he* would. The lion, driven to madness by hunger, would not continue to consider him with such a friendly eye. And even with the decline of the flood water, the span of river would be far wider than he'd be able to swim. Or row, even if the yawl were not destroyed by the charge of a new tree. It was easier, Albie discovered, to give up hope than to create or sustain it.

Well, that new house on the hill might just have to be built without his help.

That new house. New. It would be a house without a past, with only a present and a future. Would a new house promise a new life? This old house in which he now sat, staring out of what had been one of the first lift-up windows in northern Wisconsin, this old house had been nourished on myths of human endurance. And the house had communicated those myths from grandparents to parents and from parents to him. It was from that legacy that he would now have to draw the ability and will essential to survive. His grandparents had done it. His parents had done it. He would do it.

By the time he was as old as his father was now, the

new house would have composed its own myths so that *his* children would in turn have their legacy of endurance. But those myths would be *his* creations, not the creations of his parents or his grandparents.

"A pitcher," his mother had said. She'd said it then, but he heard it now. He heard it and searched the room, astonished at the exact presence of her voice and the absence of her body. "A pitcher will pour out exactly what's been put in it. Nothing else."

It had been that snowdrift night the salesman from Duluth had expanded their universe beyond the forest. He'd handed down from his wagon, from mittened hands to mittened hands, bolts of linsey-woolsey and tow linen, as well as two cooking pots and a soap kettle and a barrel of real nails and a skillet and an anvil and four framed and paned windows with their sash-weights. At the dinner table, before the lecture in front of the fire on the exotic Mississippi steamboats, he'd stressed not only the physical advantages of such windows (that could so easily be opened and closed to admit fresh air) but also the aesthetic value. His father, in reply, had said he'd never thought of a house having aesthetic value (after he'd had the salesman explain the term). A house, after all, his father had said, was not a church. And Albie's mother had said that here, in this wilderness, *that*, exactly, for *her*, was what a house was —as well as a home. Her children, she'd said, would take out to the world what this house had poured into them. His father had laughed and said she talked as if a house were a pitcher. And she'd said that yes, in a manner of speaking, she guessed that was what she'd meant. "A pitcher," she'd said, "will pour out exactly what's been poured into it. Nothing else."

Albie closed his eyes and shook his head, to help the sound of his mother's voice complete its escape. He opened his eyes and looked out of the window that had been broken by the jars Big Rafe and Frederick had hurled. The window was admitting not rain but sunlight, not a cold wind but a balmy breeze sweet with the scent of leaves and buds, and bright and buoyant with, suddenly, the unfamiliar calls of one, two unfamiliar birds. As Albie tried to locate . . . there went a flash of red and yellow . . . the birds through that grill of branches, he saw again the distant hills, the trees, and, beyond the trees, hazy and remote, a green meadow, and beyond the meadow, on hills even more remote, the irregular dark shape of a forest.

Was it an illusion of the late afternoon light or was the land closer? A half mile away. Not, Albie estimated, much more than that. In a day or two days, as the water continued to go down and more and more land continued to be exposed, the land would continue to approach the island.

The sun was low in the sky. He'd have to hurry to bring the two goats from the yawl before dark. He'd tie them in his mother's workroom, or in what had been Elizabeth and Alice Anne's room. Then, tomorrow, he'd clean the room again—in case he had to stay.

"You thought . . ."

Albie's clothes seemed to billow out from his body,

and his skin seemed to billow with them as the voice was followed by the click of a hammer in, Albie knew, a rifle.

". . . we'd leave you behind, didn't you?"

Albie heard the "tee hee" before he turned to face Big Rafe. Shifting from one foot to another, Spider, behind Big Rafe, continued to giggle. Both men held rifles.

"Remember, Big Rafe," Spider whined. "You promised."

"I know, I know."

"No killin'. It's bad luck. Frederick was a warnin'. I'm not church-going, but . . ."

"I told you I *know!*"

And Spider, convulsively nodding his head and twitching his shoulders, retreated behind the wall, to the right of the door.

"Where's the yawl?" Big Rafe asked.

"It was smashed by a tree."

"You're lyin'."

"I'm not. That's why there's no food here except that one crate. That's all I saved."

Big Rafe seemed uncertain. His heavy brows set in deep furrows as he considered what Albie had said. Then his eyes were caught by the rope Albie had constructed from his mother's strips of cloth. The pile of rope, still damp, lay in the corner of the room. Big Rafe picked it up and examined it, grunting and mumbling to himself. "Spider."

"Yeah, Big Rafe?" Spider popped into the room.

"I got an idea."

162

"You said we was still gonna hold him for . . ."

"That thing you call a boat can hardly carry two people."

"Right, Big Rafe. I didn't have time . . ."

"You're gonna row me back. Then you're gonna come back here for him, and you're gonna row him back to the boat."

"Big Rafe, that's a lot of rowin'. The river's down, but that current's still . . ."

Big Rafe ignored Spider's protests as he'd ignored Frederick's a few days before. He leaned his rifle against the wall and stood at the side of the chair Albie was sitting in. He pounded the chair with his fist, tested the upholstery, tried to wriggle the frame. Then he stretched out a portion of the rope.

"Now," Big Rafe said. "You try escapin' while we're gone and you're through. I'll toss you in the river. You hear me?"

"You promised," Spider reminded him, his voice near tears.

"You hear me?" Big Rafe asked again.

Albie nodded.

"And, Spider, you let this boy pull anything on you, well, you might think I can't run that boat alone, but I just might try it."

Spider trapped the giggles inside his mouth with one grimy hand. "Big Rafe, you don't know which end of the boiler the steam comes out of. You'd probably put water in the firebox and wood in the . . ." He turned very serious and obedient when Big Rafe, interrupting

163

his efforts to tie Albie in the chair, indicated he saw nothing comic in Spider's comments. Spider hurried forward, offering his services. When Big Rafe waved him aside, Spider offered his services to Albie. "Look at it this way. You come with us, peaceful, you'll get back home. Try and escape and you'll end up in the river, face down. You get what I mean? Tee hee, he gets it, Big Rafe."

Big Rafe circled the chair several times with the rope, setting the final knot in place at the back of the chair.

Big Rafe picked up his rifle. "Let's go."

"Anything in the house worth takin'?" Spider asked.

"Nah. Frederick went through it before. There's nothin'."

"Poor old Frederick," Spider said. "I never will forget . . ."

"You better start tryin'. Let's go."

"All right, all right, Big Rafe. But I sure don't like all that rowin'. But if you say so . . ."

"I say so. Let's go."

They left the room and went up the hallway, in the direction of the hole Albie had tried to cover with the dresser. "This piece," Spider said. "This would draw a pretty price in Vicksburg, Big Rafe. Shame we can't haul it aboard. First-class piece of cabinetwork." Albie did not hear the response to Spider's suggestion.

Big Rafe had done his work well. After twenty minutes of squirming and struggling, Albie had not slackened one rope. His only alternative was to outwit Spider somehow after he was untied. He stopped struggling and tried to relax, to conserve his strength. If he could only devise some trick that would get him Spider's gun. That was what he had to do.

A cough brought his head up. There was Alice, at the entrance of the room, sprawled half inside and half out in the hallway.

"Alice," Albie said. "Go away. Run. Hide. He'll shoot you."

Unimpressed, the lion chewed at her right paw, licked it, and chewed it again. With a grunt, she fell onto her side, licked the pad of her left paw, and began to wash her face.

"Alice," he said, his voice sharp. "Hide! Go *hide!*" She continued washing her face. Then, because, finally, Albie had to expel all those doubts and fears that had been collecting inside him since the first morning he realized he was adrift on the Mississippi River, he tilted back his head and screamed one long outburst of rage and frustration, of rage and despair, of rage and denunciation. One, two, three, four long outbursts, but each less severe, less demanding of throat and lungs than the one before. Then he waited, panting, his throat throbbing. He let his chin drop onto his chest. He wanted to weep but could dredge up neither the energy nor the resources for tears.

At his first outburst, Alice had leaped erect. Then, throughout the next three, she simply sat and observed Albie. Now, as he grew silent, she lay down again, only to rise, a growl deep in her chest. She went up the hall and promptly returned, her ears tight against her head, her lips twitching, her belly so low that it swept the floor. She crept down the hall toward the steps that led to the kitchen.

A few minutes later Spider appeared at the door of the room, his rifle in his hands. "Tee hee. So you're still tied up, huh? Big Rafe knows his knots, don't he?"

Spider leaned his rifle against the wall, drew a large penknife from his pocket, opened it, and cut the cloth rope, leaving the hands and feet to be freed last. He stepped back fast to retrieve his rifle.

"Let's go," Spider said. "We ain't got too much time before dark. You're gonna row. Tee hee. You got that yawl over here on your own, you oughta be able to get us back. Come on. I talked Big Rafe into not throwin' you into the river, but you try tricks on me and you'll be sorry. Understand?"

"I understand," Albie said. As he left the room, with Spider behind him, he permitted himself one quick glance to his left. He saw the landing and, though he was not certain, he thought he saw, above the landing, the tufts of two ears and the dome of a furry skull.

"Let's go, let's go."

Spider prodded him through the hole in the wall and down the tree trunk. After four or five minutes of travel through the trees, stepping from trunk to trunk, branch to branch, they reached the border of the island. "Surprised?" Spider asked, cackling like a banty rooster.

A boat was tied to a branch. Part raft, part canoe, part yawl, it was built of sheets of tin ingeniously interlocked and caulked with heavy grease. Two oarlocks of wood had been bolted to the sides. Two wooden boxes, barely wide enough to hold one man, served as seats.

"Small," Spider said, "but she floats. Tee hee. Made it in four hours. Pretty little thing, ain't she? Get in."

Spider faced the boat, so he could keep his eyes on Albie, while he kneeled and fumbled with the rope. Albie, about to lower himself from the tree and into the boat, heard the growl first.

"What was that?" Spider said. "That you?"

Alice, belly low, was creeping along an overhanging branch.

"Spider," Albie said, hoping to distract him, "I can't row. You'll have to show me how."

"Look here, you. You rowed that . . ." He stopped talking to turn his head. "Somethin's goin' on. You got some trick cooked up? I'm warnin' you, boy." When he leveled his rifle at Albie, Alice, with a snarl, sprang onto the limb Spider was standing on. Spider whirled as the limb dipped. It sprang back, propelling him through the air and into the water near the ends of the branches. The rifle fell in the water close to the boat, and Albie grabbed it before it could sink.

Flapping his arms and sputtering, Spider grabbed at the branches, but they broke off in his fingers as he caught them. Alice, a constant rumble in her throat, moved from one limb to another, until she was close enough to reach down and swing her left front paw.

Spider screamed. He went under the water and came back up, five deep gashes across his temple and right cheek. "Shoot him!" he pleaded. "Kill him!"

Albie held the rifle for a moment, balancing it with right hand on the grip and left hand high on the stock. "Oh, for Chrissake, kill him, *kill him!*"

Albie reached back and threw the rifle as far as he could. It sailed through the air and dropped, muzzle first, into the water. He watched the water rise up in a splash and settle. "Here," he called. "Grab the boat."

He untied the rope, and he shoved the boat clear of the branches, toward the choking, screaming Spider.

Alice, waiting patiently for one more opportunity, stretched out on the limb, still growling.

Spider caught the edge of the tin, and after several efforts to throw his leg up over, he finally succeeded. Still spilling and shaking water from his body, he hurried the boat out of range of the lion's claw. The five gashes were bleeding now, but Spider was laughing. "Well," he called, "we won't get no ransom, but at least we don't have to worry about you gettin' back to land. Tee hee. Hope that panther don't get no stomachache from chewin' on you." And, still giggling, Spider devoted his efforts to fighting the current and returning to the *Delta Belle.*

Albie turned to find Alice. She was gone.

CHAPTER 12

Albie had little difficulty finding his way back to the yawl, but twice, while rushing from one limb to another, he slipped on moss-covered bark. He saved himself from falling into the brown water by catching onto other limbs.

At the yawl, he untied the two goats and started back, leading each one on a separate rope. Both goats were small, and though they'd been fed recently, they were still lethargic. Heads down, breathing heavily, they stumbled frequently as they followed him. When, suddenly, the twilight silence was shattered by a heavy blast and a whistle, and a thick column of black smoke shot up into the air, one of the goats panicked. It dropped, to hang above the water, twisting and gasping at the end of its rope. Albie laid the other rope down, stood on it, and hauled up the goat. It had almost choked itself to death.

Farther on, in a break in the wall of trees, Albie saw the *Delta Belle*. Its rotating wheels spilled streams of water into the dying light. Black smoke climbing from its stack caught the last faint glow of orange radiating up across the dome of the sky by the sun now fallen below the horizon. The name, *Delta Belle*, was almost but not quite lost.

The boat moved down the river, to disappear again behind a thick clot of trees. Albie hurried toward the house. Then, again, there she was, framed in a clearing in the branches, her wheels churning the brown water, converting it from muddy brown to white, sparkling foam. The stack continued to spill the thick black smoke. Long after Albie could no longer see the boat, the smoke continued to climb the sky, to hang like a storm cloud, to thin, to fade, finally to be dispersed by the breeze.

Albie reached the house and led the two animals up the tree and through the wall and down the hallway into his mother's workroom. As if they'd made some solemn pact during the trip to collapse the moment they arrived, the goats promptly lay down and closed their eyes.

Albie tied their ropes to snags of broken studs, knowing that if Alice needed food, one or both of the goats would be dead when he returned from the next trip. Well, he'd brought them for her, so it made little difference whether she killed them now or later. He stroked one head and then the other. His heart went out to the stupid animals. If he could, he would protect them as he would, he knew, protect Alice. He tried to think about order, about choices, about certain things being more necessary than other things, but the chain of thought was too complex. All he knew was that it was not easy. He wanted to put his arms around their scrawny necks and try to explain his dilemma to them. But how could he when he couldn't even explain it to himself? Would he ever again, he wondered, be able to so much as withdraw the barbed hook from the gills of a fish? Would he be able ever again to stand with idle apathy as his father drew the gleaming knife blade across the throat of a screaming sow?

When he left the house for the next trip to the yawl, Alice was standing on the tree trunk, waiting for him. Sometimes preceding him, sometimes falling behind, she leaped from tree to tree like a playful house cat. He passed under a heavy branch at one especially difficult part of the passage and almost lost his footing when a paw appeared in front of his face and then, next to the paw, the upended face of the lion. She made two pretentiously awkward jabs at his head and galloped on, to climb another limb, where she again waited for him to pass beneath so she could repeat her game.

More than once they were so close that he could have

reached out and touched her body. He didn't, not because he didn't want to but because he knew that, though there was a bond between them, that bond was tentative and dared not be tested yet.

When they returned to the house, Alice paused to sniff the air. Albie waited, knowing she smelled the goats. If she intended to go to the workroom, he did not want to be there to witness the kill. But apparently satisfied that they'd be there when she wanted them, she gave a tentative grunt, and, with a switch of her tail, she continued to her room.

In his room, Albie looked out of the window and across the river. The nearest hills were just barely visible. Hills, he thought, Alice and her cubs would never prowl. The cubs. Before the last light was gone, he had to see them. He'd not seen them since the day they'd been born, and now, as he watched the faint lines of the hills growing fainter, as he thought of the cubs never feeling the bark of those trees, never gliding through that tall grass, his heart ached for their loss.

Alice, lying on her side, lifted her head when Albie appeared. She seemed about to rise, about to spit, but then her head fell back and she seemed to doze while the cubs mauled and nipped her chin and throat. They dug at her nipples, they climbed up one side to her back and tumbled down the opposite side to land with a thump on the floor, to lie there for a moment, out of sight. Then, mewing, they struggled up that smooth mountain of brown fur again (ears appeared, then eyes, then grinning, whimpering muzzles) to slide down the silky flanks, to tumble again, to whimper and dash for a few quick drinks at those rosy fountains that promised to be available forever.

Albie was tempted to move closer, to pick up one of the cubs, but he knew, again, his and the lion's alliance was too tenuous to permit such intimacy.

But oh, how he envied those two fur balls the soft fur-covered belly of their mother, that shelter of the curved forepaw. He wanted so much to curl up in the near darkness with them, to receive the beauty and security of her easy power. If he could have one wish now, it would be to join these cubs, to glide with them through those remote green hills, to sleep with them in caves and trees.

Close, and edging closer, Albie, if he wanted to, could reach out and touch the rump of the nearest cub. But he didn't. Not yet.

Except for her eyes, which were open and observing his hands, his feet, his own eyes, Alice did not move. Albie paused, to wait until Alice's eyes closed again, and then, again, he moved. Her eyes opened and a sound, a heavy purr or a low growl, oozed from the lion's throat, and her head came up from the floor and fell again, eyes almost closed. Almost.

Albie's thumb touched, rubbed, the base of the stubby tail of one of the cubs. The cub mewed and Albie pulled his hand back, and Alice, with a spit and a snarl, was standing on all fours, tumbling the astonished cubs to the floor. She crouched, her jaws half open, inches from Albie's throat. Albie closed his eyes. When he opened

173

them, Alice, sitting, was examining his face, her own face again a perfect image of Albie's sister, Alice Anne, at those moments when she'd stare at the world, perplexed, after a spanking.

"Alice Anne," Albie said.

The lion cocked her head to one side.

"You are, you really are Alice Anne."

The lion blinked and settled to her belly, within reach of Albie's right hand, which he did not move.

"I'll tell her all about you. I'll tell her stories when I sit beside her bed in the dark."

The head cocked and tilted again and her brow furled. Albie giggled. The head cocked to the right and then to the left; the eyes focused on Albie's mouth from which, again, came a chuckle and then a guarded laugh.

The lion's head came forward, her eyes gleaming yellow in the darkness that fell now almost with a hard, swishing sound. The moist nose hesitated just beyond the reach of Albie's hand, almost touched the skin. Her warm breath tickled his wrist.

When the surface of the lion's nose touched the surface of Albie's hand, her head jerked back, as if she'd been stung. Her head again moved forward. Her nostrils scouted the terrain of Albie's wrist. The thick, pebble-covered tongue rolled out to test, to taste, and then to lick the skin of finger, hand, and wrist.

Albie lay back, flat on the floor. He felt the skin scraped from his wrist, and he turned his hand over. He moved his fingertips, rubbing, scratching, the underside of the chin. Purring, Alice raised her head to expose her throat, so Albie's fingers could dig at the furrow in the soft fur where that leather belt had once circled her neck.

He would have slept there, happily, had a single bleat not sounded from the room where the goats were tied. Albie slid his hand out from under Alice's throat, and he backed away. He stepped out into the night, felt his way along the tree and in through the other opening and down the hall to his mother's workroom. He fumbled his way about the dark room until he found the goats. They were still lying on the floor, but they were panting heavily. Maybe, Albie decided, they were hungry or thirsty.

He was reluctant to give up any of the little food he had, knowing that tomorrow, when he'd go to recover the rest of the food in the yawl, food and yawl might both be gone. But he'd not be able to sleep tonight knowing the goats were starving.

There was one pint jar in the crate he'd brought from the yawl. He opened it, drank some of the fluid, and discovered, with his tongue, that the jar was filled with long green beans. When he held the jar in front of their noses (after feeling, first, to make sure it was their noses), each goat ate a few beans, and one of the two tasted the juice, once.

Back in the chair in his room, Albie listened to the branches rubbing and clicking against each other. Another night. But tonight he'd sleep better than he'd slept the preceding nights. He'd not be frightened, tonight, of floating into the Gulf or into the Atlantic Ocean, he'd not

175

be fearing an attack from the lion, he'd not be hiding from Big Rafe and Frederick and Spider.

When Albie awakened and discovered both goats lying with legs outstretched, dead, he thought that Alice had killed them. But there was not a spot of blood. Their bodies, not yet stiff or cold, did not contain a single claw or tooth mark. Since both goats were still warm, they might, Albie thought, still be acceptable to the lion.

When he lifted the larger of the two bodies, Albie glanced out the window. Those green hills had surely marched toward the island during the night. The river must surely have gone down several more feet.

This time, when he entered Alice's room, he was not greeted with a snarl or a growl. She was probably back in the closet with her cubs. After depositing the goat near the closet opening, Albie said, "Alice, here's a gift." When she still did not appear, Albie moved closer, sliding the goat before him with his foot. He stepped back, so she'd not suspect he was planning to steal her cubs. Still no sign of her.

Something was wrong. Deciding to chance her wrath, Albie stepped inside. The closet was empty. She'd taken her cubs . . . but there, in the farthest corner, a little ball of fur grumbled and spit at him, probably furious at its inability to obey its mother's strict command to remain silent and concealed. Where had she taken the other cub?

Albie ran out of the house, crawled over one branch, one tree after another, trying to discover the new nest

Alice had made or selected. Had she reconsidered her and Albie's demonstration of mutual trust last night and decided, this morning, that her cubs would be more secure out of the reach of Albie's hands? If she'd reconsidered, if she was building a nest, it would have to be in one of the trees. But surely she'd sense the dangers of a tree above a rushing river. Perhaps the risk of death for her cubs was more desirable than were the consequences of a friendship with a man.

It was almost noon when he reached the area where the yawl had been. It was gone. He found a piece of it, with the oarlock and oar still attached, in the root ball of a poplar tree that had smashed into the island sometime during the night. That meant that he now had only the few jars of food that were in the crate in his room.

Near evening he gave up and returned, saddened and defeated, to the house. Wherever it was, Alice had successfully concealed the nest—an obvious indication that she did not want him near her cubs, and perhaps not even near her. He'd honor her needs, he'd not continue his search, he'd not force her to abide by what *he* considered safe. The cubs would be taking their chances with death soon enough; they might as well learn to take those chances now.

In his room, Albie forced himself to sip at the juice in a jar of corn. He'd go to Alice's room, not to touch the cub but only to assure it that it had not been deserted. If Alice did not return the next morning to carry this cub to her new nest, well, he'd have to assume that both Alice and her cub had somehow fallen into the river and been swept away. He'd have to feed the cub, or try to feed it. Then he thought of the dead goat still in the next room. He replaced the lid on the jar. Before he visited the cub, he'd dispose of the goat.

He dragged it to the shattered wall of the workroom and threw the stiff body into the river. It floated into a net of branches, was pulled free by the current, was caught and held by several strips of bailing wire, and then, again floating free, it dipped under a wall of tangled brush and vines and disappeared.

Because of the heat, it would be wise to dispose also of the goat he'd left in Alice's room. When he crawled over the frame, or what was left of the frame where the window had been, there was Alice lying near the entry to the closet, her cub slurping at the nipple, kneading the pink flesh with its oversized paws. The eviscerated carcass of the goat lay on the floor.

Albie was restrained from rushing forward to hug Alice not so much by his own sense of caution as by the sound of her growl. It was not a gentle purr, it was an undeniably warning growl, which stopped when Albie contented himself with a seat on the floor nearby. Her coat was soaked, her paws were caked with mud. She had probably fallen into the river, had probably lost her cub. That had to be why she was now so sullen.

Albie returned to the room three times during the day and each time found the lion asleep, with the cub enjoying its solitary possession of its mother. The last two times he came, Albie brought Alice a pan of water from the river. She sipped it, licked her chin and nose, pulled some of the caked mud from between her pads, and then flopped down again, to sleep. It had, obviously, been an exhausting ordeal.

Albie toured the island twice in the afternoon, hoping to find a few remnants from the yawl. Even a few jars might make the difference. But he found nothing. The humming brown water, still delivering flood refuse to the island, was dropping noticeably, exposing bodies of a variety of animals trapped in the roots and branches. Bloated, beginning to decompose in the hot sun, they were contaminating the air with an odor even more foul than the odor on the *Delta Belle*. That evening, from his chair at the window, with Alice stretched out at his feet, Albie gauged the distance between the island and the land. Four hundred yards at the most. The river must almost be down to normal. It might go down another five or ten feet, but not much more than that. The top mud lines on the trees were about twenty feet above the still swift surface of the water. Another five feet would, he guessed, mean the approach of another fifty yards of land.

Why hadn't he thought to bring tools when he'd escaped from the *Delta Belle?* With an ax he could make a raft and at least try to pole across the river. Or rope. Why hadn't he brought one of those coils of rope he'd left in the boat's boiler room? He could have tied scattered branches together for the crossing. But with neither ax nor rope, he had no chance.

So he had no alternative but to wait for the boats to start running up the river again, to start the destruction of the island of snags that now stretched at least a quarter of a mile in length.

That night, again, Albie slept peacefully. The next morning, when he went to her room, both Alice and her other cub were gone.

That, Albie decided, was the end of Alice. He'd probably never see her again. Which, he forced himself to admit, was probably for the best.

He had little time to brood about it. Within minutes after discovering their disappearance, Albie heard three shrill whistles. At the far end of the island, a boat was steaming up the river.

It took an hour, perhaps two hours, for Albie to cross the island. By the time he reached the last snag and perched there, the boat was far upstream, sounding its whistle. But, Albie knew, if there were one, there was bound to be another. He took off his shirt and tied it to a long branch from which he cleaned all the leaves and twigs. He waited, watching the water until his eyes ached from the bright sunlight and his stomach began to rebel both from the lack of food and the aroma of rotting flesh and baked mud.

Late that afternoon the blast of a whistle forced his eyes open. He'd been napping. There, far out in the water, a trim stern-wheeler was smoking her way up the river. She was too far away for Albie to read her name, but he kept calling, "Hey, I'm over here, I'm over here," as he waved his shirt flag back and forth, around and around.

The boat continued, blasting its whistle, shooting its

smoke into the sky, until it disappeared around a bend.

Late, near dusk, Albie returned to his house. He drank the juice from a jar of tomatoes and ate most of the pulp. His shoulders and back and face were badly burned, and he soaked his shirt in the water several times during the night so he might wrap himself and sleep in relative comfort. He was disappointed, but he knew that someone on one of the boats (and there would be more boats every day), someone was bound to see him.

He awakened before dawn. His shoulders and back were blistered. He sat up to see the sky changing from black to rose. A bird sang outside the window. Another bird replied, from another tree. Albie swung his feet out of bed and almost stepped on Alice, who leaped up with a growl and moved aside.

The odor of her wet fur filled the room. She went to the door and returned and went back to the door, short, coughing grunts accompanying each step. Her pads left faintly damp prints on the floor.

Albie, at first, felt almost sad to see the lion again. He'd begun that long adjustment to her desertion. But now, seeing her, he was happy enough to almost forget the pain of his burned back and shoulders.

"What is it, Alice? What? Did you bring them back? Did you change your mind?"

She left his room, went up the hall, returned, and once more went up the hall, still grunting.

Albie followed her, thinking she was leading him to her cubs. Out through the window hole, onto the sloping tree, down the trunk, to the water that lapped at the twigs and trunks and branches. She kept looking back, and when she was sure he was following her, she went on. At the edge of the water she looked back again, stepped into the water, and, stretching out her neck, started swimming toward the land visible now in the red-orange sunrise.

After swimming a short distance, Alice looked back. She returned, glared at Albie, cough-growling, and then she swam away again. She returned, this time her grunts sharp, fierce. She paced back and forth between him and the water, her head swinging.

Albie knew now where she'd gone with her cubs. And he also knew why she'd returned this time. His heart seemed to melt inside his chest. There was no way to acknowledge his love now except to respond. If he waited, just one or two more days, he would be rescued. There was not the slightest doubt in his mind. But Alice was offering him what she considered to be his last chance for escape *now*—this minute. If he tried to swim that distance, he knew he'd not make it. He would be killing himself simply to demonstrate to a dumb wild beast his gratitude for her trust. Albie looked back once at the house. He listened for the sound of a steam whistle. In the silence, he walked down the trunk and stepped out into the water and began to move his arms, stroking leisurely, waiting to feel his body sink. He closed his eyes and refused to recognize their faces . . . Elizabeth's . . . Alice Anne's . . .

His right hand, at the crest of a stroke, struck a limb,

a soft limb, and his fingers closed about it. His other hand reached, caught the same soft limb, and gripped and held. He was being pulled. He opened his eyes and saw Alice's back in front of him, her head and shoulders high out of the water, her front legs pumping. Albie clutched desperately at her tail, his arms feeling as if they were being tugged from their sockets. Then, relaxing his muscles and kicking his feet, he discovered that his efforts not only eased the punishment to his shoulders and back but actually helped the thrust of the lion through the water. By careful coordination of arms and legs, he eased the drag on Alice, so she could move with greater speed and less effort.

When they reached the shallows, the lion let down her feet. Albie did the same. He sank to his knees in the soft mud. But he was standing. He was *standing*— standing near the shore.

They waited there in the shallow water, in the mud, resting. Then, when the lion sloshed through the water toward the low, sloping bank, Albie staggered after her, falling several times, rising, continuing toward the land.

The mud grew progressively more solid. When he reached the bank, Albie managed to claw his way up the slope. After he slid his body over the crest, he lay on the grass. He watched a hawk circling, gliding on the faint orange wind.

He sat up. Alice was sitting, panting, a few feet from him. Then, as if she'd completed her final responsibility, she gazed longingly, impatiently, toward the remote hills and the even more remote forest. She glanced once more at Albie, and, without so much as a whisper or a grunt, she walked away. Her long stride eased into a casual lope.

The last Albie saw of her, the last he was ever to see of her, was her long, lean body loping directly into the morning's rusty sun. He watched her move across the flat meadow, he watched until her body diminished to a speck, and he continued watching until that speck was swallowed by that rusty mouth of the rising sun.

AN AFTERWORD

Albie left his room on the *James Donahue* twice in three days for feeble attempts to eat.

At Galena he changed to the *Dennis Hall*. Two days later he arrived in St. Paul. During his almost two days on the *Dennis Hall* he left his room once, to eat a dinner that stayed with him less than an hour. At St. Paul, Albie boarded a stagecoach which, eighteen hours later, stopped at a small hills village called Chippewa.

So weak he could barely stand and sore in every muscle and bone, Albie climbed down from the stage. When he tried to run and couldn't, he was swept up into the arms of his teary-eyed, husky-voiced father who'd been waiting at the side of Albie's buckskin mare, Summer.

During the ride home in the wagon, Albie and his father talked very little. Albie slept much of the time and pretended to sleep the rest. His father commented three or four times on those good people, the Townsends, in Vicksburg. He and Albie's mother, he assured Albie, had written the Townsends, thanking them for their kindness during Albie's recuperation and preparation for the long trip home. They'd assured the Townsends that they would somehow manage to repay the money the Townsends had spent but would probably never have the opportunity to repay their Christian love.

Albie's father did most of the talking. He described in detail the new house he and the Abernathy boys were building. He listed and described, in detail, the animals they'd purchased to replace those lost in the flood, and he thanked God for the Abernathys and reminded Albie that as long as a man had neighbors like the Abernathys, as long as there were kind people like the Townsends in this country, this country had nothing to worry about.

Near evening, Albie began to recognize the land. He pointed out the hill where he and Elizabeth had picked the giant blackberries. And there, under that birch, was where he'd been attacked by wasps. And there, in the creek, he'd learned to swim. After the last reminiscence Albie leaned back in the seat of the wagon, watched the rhythmic movement of Summer's muscles, and slept.

An hour later he awakened to hear a dog barking. His father slowed Summer to a walk, and Albie, the word "Shep" in his throat but not yet at his lips, stepped down to the road.

The dog leaped and growled and whined and licked Albie's face, and Albie laughed and danced and hugged the dog, and for the first time Albie's father said that yes, the dog could ride in the wagon seat with Albie. But just this one time. A dog shouldn't be spoiled. A spoiled dog gets confused about who's the master.

For Albie the last mile of the dirt road was the longest of the thirty miles he and his father had traveled together. After seven weeks almost to the day he was coming home.

Coming home? His home was gone. A new home was being built.

Coming home? He wanted to ask his father to take the time to drive to the new house, so he could at least see it, but his father's face, beaming with pleasure and pride, was concentrating on the road. He let out a laugh as Summer broke into a trot. Albie settled back, to lean against Shep.

The wagon rounded a curve in the road, and there, at the bottom of a gently sloping green valley, lay the Abernathy farm. In the yard, near the front porch: a cluster of seven or eight people. He was not sure which of the two women was his mother. The other, smaller, figure in a dress could only be Elizabeth. But there could be no doubt who that was in the green dress with hair like Summer's sun-struck mane, her little butterball body hopping up and down.

Summer drew the wagon through the gate, up the long winding rock-edged drive toward the gray board barn and the gray house beyond. Albie stood, ready to leap down the moment they entered the last stretch before the front gate. As they passed the barn, with Summer stepping high and snorting and Shep barking and slapping Albie's legs with his tail, Albie fell back in his seat and covered his eyes with his arms so he might not continue to see that huge (shaped like a mammoth brown bat in flight) freshly stripped pelt of a mountain lion, stretched taut, tacked to the boards.

The carriage stopped, and there were shouts of "Albie . . . he's here . . . there he is . . " and Shep darted in and out of running legs, his barks drowned out by shouts and laughter.

Albie remained in his seat, his body rigid, his face in his hands. His father lifted him out of the wagon and stood him on his feet. He would have crumpled to the ground had his father not continued to hold him erect. The laughter, the shouting and cheering, stopped. Only Shep continued his joyous, frenzied welcome.

"He's still sick," his mother said, sobbing and rushing forward to kneel before him, to embrace him, to hold his face in her hands, to examine him. "They said he was better, he was well enough to travel . . . Albie . . . Albie, son. Are you sick? Do you want to go in and lie down?" When Albie, his fists grinding his eyes, did not respond, she turned to Albie's father. "He doesn't hear me. What's happened to him?" She tried to draw his hands from his eyes, and when that failed, she threw her arms around him again and pulled his body into her arms. "What's happened to my son?" she cried, tears spilling into and out of her eyes.

Alice Anne broke free of Elizabeth's hand and ran across the grass. She stood in front of Albie, tugging at his shirt, grinning up at him through a recently acquired smear of raspberry jam.

Albie worked free of his mother's arms and walked back to the barn. He stood in front of the cougar pelt. It was still dripping blood.

With a groan that exploded into a howl that silenced Shep, Albie began to weep. Hoarse sobs tore themselves from his chest. He dropped to his knees, his body jerking under the tyranny of his sobbing, and all those who'd been standing in the yard shuffled down the road to hover in bewildered silence behind him. Shep lay in front of Albie, peering up into his face, waiting.

He was still weeping when Alice Anne came to him, to tug at one hand. "Don't cry, Albie."

Albie fought to control his sobs and finally permitted Alice Anne to draw one hand away from his eyes.

"I got two new teeth," Alice Anne said. "Here."

He felt his finger drawn into and through the sticky lips. The tip of his finger slid along a moist warm inner cheek and stopped at a swelling in the gum that was just beginning to break, like a willow bud about to burst into bloom.

"There," Alice Anne said. "Feel it? It's new. You want to feel the other one, Albie?"

Albie turned to confront Alice Anne. And Elizabeth and his mother and father. And the Abernathys.